DANGER IN THE AIR

MYDWORTH MYSTERIES #6

Neil Richards • Matthew Costello

RED DOG

UK

1.

A PERFECT DAY FOR FLYING

AMELIA EARHART SQUINTED, looking up at the stunningly bright sun, sitting in the deepest of blue skies.

Could not be a better day to be in the skies of England, she thought.

And she'd be there soon enough once the formalities here on the ground were taken care of.

The thought of the imminent radio interview made her feel uncomfortable. She never felt this way piloting a plane.

But standing here in front of a BBC microphone, just waiting – the slightest of breezes blowing her short hair – this was scary.

All she *really* wanted to do was walk over to the Sandbourne Aviation *Firefly*, hop into the single-seater, and take off.

Because that was just it, wasn't it? To take off, as if she was escaping – not just the place, the people, the responsibilities, the expectations – but the very planet itself.

Up there, everything looked different. Distant, yet so beautiful. Normal life carrying on below while she sailed above it all.

Was there anything better?

But for now, Amelia waited as the gnome-like engineer from the BBC fiddled with a black box attached to electrical cables, getting all set to capture her words before her departure.

Hovering over him, impatiently, the owl-eyed radio reporter who was going to conduct the live interview gave her an optimistic wave.

"All *set*, Miss Earhart!" he said. "Won't be a moment now!"

Amelia nodded. She had butterflies.

She looked to her right, where a crowd waited to see her take off. The Great Western Aerodrome, just a few miles west of London, was like most English airfields she'd seen so far on this trip – not much more than a grassy field and a couple of hangars.

But it seemed there were big plans in store for the place. Hard to imagine on this bright, sunny morning, with just a few biplanes parked up, and no hint of a decent coffee.

She turned and looked left. There sat the brilliant yellow Rolls-Royce supplied by Sandbourne, who had sponsored her trip over from the States.

Lounging against the hood, fedora tipped back, cigarette in hand, stood Wallace Smythe, the commercial agent who'd been forced upon her by Sandbourne.

His sole reason for existence seemed to be to take as big a cut as he could from the proceeds of her country-wide tour.

Back home, since her first barnstorming days, Amelia hadn't really trusted anybody to organise the flights, the schedule, the stops.

But here on this hop-scotching tour around the English countryside, she didn't have a choice. She'd been told that Smythe was indispensable. Word was, without Smythe there'd be no bookings, no tour and – most importantly – no fundraising.

Wonder whose pockets he's lining apart from his own, thought Amelia, watching him in his sweat-stained shirt sleeves, his expansive stomach eager to pop the shirt's buttons, looking about as uncomfortable as a man could in the summer heat.

Also looking on, standing at the back of the Rolls, was her sister Muriel – her beloved "Pidge", as the family had called her since she was a toddler.

And standing rather close to her, the American journalist Ronald Greene.

2

He was the man hired to file the regular stories about Amelia's English trip.

But he also seemed to have taken a rather strong interest in Pidge.

And with his dark good looks, easy smile, and also… what was the word?

Yes – she thought – *glibness.*

She wasn't too sure how she felt about his interest in her sister.

"All *right*," the radio interviewer said, hurrying over to adjust the plate-sized microphone. "Nearly there, Miss Earhart!"

Amelia nodded. Sooner this was done, the sooner she could take off, into that beautiful blue sky.

"AND WE ARE *live* in five, four, three…"

The interviewer held up fingers, counting down until the microphone, standing ominously in front of her, would be "live".

She felt a tightness in her stomach.

This was something she never experienced in the skies above.

"Two, one… and…"

Then the reporter leaned in to the microphone.

"Good afternoon, everybody. We are broadcasting to you *live* from London's famous Great Western Aerodrome, and with us is the world-famous aviatrix, Amelia Earhart! Miss Earhart would you like to say hello to our listeners!"

Amelia nodded, then felt silly. It wasn't like anyone with their radio sets could see.

Why was this so hard?

"Oh, yes! Hello everybody."

"Jolly *good*! Now can you tell everyone exactly what you are doing flying this wonderful British plane around the beautiful English countryside?"

"Ah well, I'm, uh, very lucky to have been loaned the *Firefly* here, by Sandbourne Aviation, and I've spent the last two weeks flying around your beautiful country—"

"You didn't fly your own plane here, I gather? I imagine that old pond does rather get in the way!"

"Well, yes, I haven't flown solo across the Atlantic – yet. But don't you worry, I will soon!"

"Wonderful, wonderful! And you are here on a very special mission, yes? Can you tell our audience at home all about *that*?"

And this Amelia could answer.

A mission very close to her heart.

"Yes, you see, at all these stops I am raising money for the 'Ninety-Nines'." A pause. "Th-that's the new organisation I am helping found for all the woman pilots worldwide. First of its kind!"

"Most excellent. I am sure all our female listeners, snug and safe at home, admire your guts and determination."

Amelia gave a look back towards her waiting plane.

"I think it's important that flying should be open to women and girls everywhere, and that—"

"And how are you finding the *Firefly* here?" said the reporter, clearly not wanting to hear more about the Ninety-Nines or women pilots. "British engineering at its best, eh?"

Amelia instinctively looked across the grass at her plane, where final flight checks were being made, the gas bowser just driving away.

"Oh, she's an absolutely lovely plane to fly," said Amelia. "Very sensitive. Very fast, too. Sixteen cylinders, air-cooled, three hundred horse power, supercharged you see, and—"

"Yes, jolly interesting, I'm sure. Must play absolute havoc with your hair!"

"Not really, I wear a—"

"Now, Miss Earhart, do tell us, where next on your thrilling whistle-stop tour?"

"Well, I'm off to Sussex now for one final flying display at the weekend, then—"

"Back to New York on one of our great Cunard liners, I hear?"

"Er, yes. On Sunday."

"Excellent! Well it sounds to *this* reporter as if you've had the very best of British, so long may these delightful *feminine* hands across the ocean continue!"

Amelia nodded, then saw the reporter gesture hurriedly towards the microphone.

She leaned in. "Oh yes, thank you. And thanks everybody for looking after me so well."

"Marvellous! Well that's it for now, listeners, from the Great Western Aerodrome. As we wish the fabulous aviatrix Amelia Earhart a *bon voyage*!"

And the torture was over.

Time to get into the air at last.

2.

JUST ANOTHER FLIGHT

"HARRY? ANYTHING INTERESTING?"

Sir Harry Mortimer sat in a deckchair in the back garden of the Dower House; a beautiful morning for a pot of tea, and catching up with the news.

Kat was dressed in her gardening outfit, looking ready to wrangle any bush or hedge into submission.

So domestic, he thought.

"Oh, the usual. The king, God bless him, is still rather poorly. It seems China and Russia are about to go to war. Oh – and a rather impressive riot in one of your New York prisons."

"You can always count on us New Yorkers for a good riot."

"Believe such a thing played a role in your country's quest for independence! Something about tea – Boston harbour?"

She laughed and came and sat down in the black iron chair facing him. She had a single smudge of brown on her cheek.

But that too – altogether charming.

"Any news from Cairo?" she said.

"Spot of unrest."

"I miss the place sometimes, don't you?"

"The place and the people? Why yes, I do," he said. "Food too, actually. But the secrets and plots and all that? Not me. Give me my English garden and my American wife, and I count myself a *very* lucky man."

"You know, if I wasn't so dishevelled I'd lean over and give you a great big kiss for that."

"Oh, don't let a little dirt stop you."

She smiled.

Then he thought, *What about her? Was life too domestic for her?*

"And you? Missing any of that skulduggery this lovely morning?"

Kat kept her smile. *But did she hesitate a bit there?*

"No. I mean, it *was* all rather exciting. But must say, Sir Harry, you have done an excellent job of keeping me entertained right here."

"Hasn't been *too* uneventful hasn't it?"

"That's how I like life."

"Me too. And I have to say – this weekend might be rather fun. House party, lots of people flying in and out."

"Literally," said Kat. "In fact, you keeping an eye on the time, darling? Shouldn't our special guest be arriving soon?"

Harry checked his watch and sat up fast.

"Good Lord – you're right. Dammit, I was settling in for a nice snooze there."

He watched Kat gather up the tea things.

"You coming up to the manor with me?" he said, folding *The Times* then helping her carry stuff into the house. "We can take the bike – be quicker."

"Are you kidding?" said Kat. "Amelia Earhart landing at Mydworth Manor? I wouldn't miss that for the world!"

WITH THE TALL microphone finally removed, and all the official farewells and handshakes completed, Amelia hurried over to the Rolls – that brilliant yellow colour, just as she'd requested.

DANGER IN THE AIR

After all, if we're to have fun doing this – she had told the executives at Sandbourne – *then let's have some real fun!*

She saw her young sister still chatting away with Greene in the back seat.

"Pidge, you all set?" She shot a look at the journalist. "Why not sit up front, with Mr Smythe?"

She hoped her message had gotten through to Greene. But neither he nor her sister showed any sign of shifting places.

"Know where you're heading, my dear?" said Smythe from behind the wheel.

"Flight plan all sorted," said Amelia. "Mydworth Manor – sounds like something from a story book."

"One with a happy ending, I hope. Lot of money at stake this weekend, you know."

"Don't worry, Smythe," said Amelia. "I *know*."

"Landing strip should be all marked out for you. We'll be just an hour or so behind you, I expect."

She looked across at the expectant crowd, the Movietone and Pathé cameras all lined up.

"I must go. Looks like we are all set."

"Don't forget," said Smythe. "Big wave, happy face, make it *dramatic*."

Her sister smiled. "Mellie, Be safe."

"Always, Pidge."

Smythe cleared his throat. "Yes, of course, safety too, jolly good idea."

But Greene offered a different thought.

"But if you do *try* anything a little risky, Amelia, do tell me, and all our readers, later? *After* your safe landing, of course."

Amelia gave him a slight smile, though she felt little warmth for the man.

Greene was the pipeline to all the syndicated columns in newspapers back home.

So, she had to be nice to him... somewhat.

And, with that, Amelia turned again to the crowd that had been waiting behind a rope barrier, eager to see her take off.

Taking off was something she couldn't wait to do. To fly, on a perfect day like this.

It was going to be – she knew – *absolutely wonderful.*

AMELIA WALKED TOWARDS the plane, buttoning up her flight overalls.

She knew that this walk – the brave, lone woman striding towards the death-defying machine – always made for a great newspaper photo.

Sometimes a cover.

And, as Smythe never ceased telling her, covers sold papers, and papers brought interest. And interest? Well, that brought cash.

She knew he was right: so far this amazing two-week trip had earned thousands of pounds, 80% of which would go towards launching the Ninety-Nines and training other women to make this "walk" too, this historic march into the future.

All thanks to Sandbourne and the loan of their prototype fighter plane – the *Firefly*. They wanted publicity, she wanted publicity.

It was the perfect match. And the plane – with its sleek single wing, its lean, aerodynamic lines – sure was a beauty.

Though she had her eyes on a very different sort of plane when she got back to the states.

A Lockheed Vega.

That she would make sure was the *deepest* of reds.

DANGER IN THE AIR

There'd be no missing *that* as she flew around the country, or even when – and she knew the day was not far away – she crossed the Atlantic.

This time, not as a passenger, but as the *pilot*.

As she got close to the *Firefly*, her engineer, an old timer supplied by Smythe, stepped out of the cockpit.

Paddy O'Brien. One of the best, Smythe had told her.

And sure, he was good. He knew the *Firefly* backwards and forwards – a real flyer's engineer.

But when Amelia had been introduced to him two weeks back, she'd immediately noticed the tell-tale crisscross of bloodshot eyes.

And having grown up with that – with her father – the clues were not something Amelia would ever miss. Paddy O'Brien, good engineer and all, liked a tipple, and it showed.

As she reached the plane, she saw him crouch down and fiddle with the maze of pipes and wires beneath the cockpit.

"We all set, Paddy?"

"Just about, Amelia," said the engineer, not looking up. "Nearly ready for you."

Amelia picked up her flying goggles and aviator hat from the seat of the single-seater.

As she put them on, and adjusted the straps, she looked down again at O'Brien, his hands deep in the pipework.

"We got a problem?" she said.

The engineer moved back, then rose and turned to her, wiping his oily hands on a rag.

She caught an expression on his face – an expression she'd not seen on him before.

Anxiety.

"I dunno," he said. "Fuel gauge acting up."

"How?"

"Bit random. Full one minute, then empty."

10

"She's fuelled up though?"

"Two full tanks."

Amelia looked back at the waiting crowd. *Delaying was not an option.*

"Right," she said. "Can't be more than a thirty-minute flight. Got the gas. Who needs gauges? Let's go."

"You're the boss," said O'Brien, with the usual shake of her hand. Then he took the cable from the starter battery trolley and plugged it into the side of the plane.

Amelia stepped up to the wing and gave a wave to the crowd who in mere moments would all shrink to the size of dots. Then she hopped into the seat and pulled the plane door shut.

Her flight cap on tight, she buckled it under her chin as she scanned the now-familiar instruments before her.

Altimeter, air-speed indicator, compass.

The fuel gauges – both reading full.

She reached forward and pressed the button for the ignition. The engine turned, coughed – but nothing.

Amelia frowned, looked through the cockpit glass at Paddy, who wiped his forehead with the oily rag, his face serious. He nodded. She hit the button again.

And then, as if awakening from a deep sleep – like some beast in a cave stirring – the engine *coughed* as it came to life, then rumbled as the propeller began to spin, slowly at first, waiting for the pilot to pull on the throttle, to increase speed.

Amelia waited until Paddy had unhooked the cable and stepped well clear, then she reached down and released the brake, giving the array of instruments one last look before she started moving.

All looked good on this perfect flying day.

As she let go of the brake handle, she pulled back on the throttle, easy at first, just enough to get the light plane moving.

She used the tail's rudder to turn it away from the crowd that she knew would be watching her every manoeuvre.

Then – getting the *Firefly* lined up straight on the grass for take-off – she started pulling back more on the throttle, the engine's rpms going up, the great propeller moving the plane forward.

This part? Always so exciting. The magic of a plane rolling across the grass, bouncing like some oddly designed land vehicle *until…*

She held the control stick tight, picking up speed again as she gently nudged the throaty beast forward, faster.

Then, she *felt* that moment when the rubber tyres began to lose their tenuous hold on the ground, until that hold was *gone*.

Nose up slightly, the plane started to soar into the cloudless sky.

One quick look back at those waiting below – seeing their arms waving.

She waved back, but already knew – her speed now over 100 knots, hundreds of feet above the ground – that those below probably couldn't see her in the cockpit at all.

Just this agile plane, soaring upwards, heading south, to the land and skies of Sussex, to the quaint-sounding Mydworth Manor.

3.

A FALL FROM THE HEAVENS

KAT STOOD WITH Harry and Lady Lavinia, on the rear terrace of Mydworth Manor, looking out at the improvised landing ground, where the grass of the meadows had been cut as short as the gardener Grayer could make it.

"I *do* hope nobody ends up in the lake this weekend," said Lavinia.

"Don't worry, Lavinia," said Harry. "Planes these days do have brakes, you know."

"So did your very first car, Harry. But, if you remember, that didn't prevent you from nearly disappearing beneath the waters on your twenty-first."

"Now there's a story you haven't told me, Harry," said Kat.

"Hardly broke the surface, as I remember it," said Harry. "And so long ago, who can remember the details?"

"I can," Lavinia said, grinning.

Harry must have been a handful for her, thought Kat. *Yet her affection for him? Undeniable.*

"Anyway, Lavinia, the landing strip is perfectly long enough."

"Good," said Lavinia. "I believe we're now expecting at least half a dozen planes tomorrow. Heaven knows where they'll park."

"All under control, don't you worry," said Harry. "Should be quite a display."

"Long as they don't bump into each other," said Lavinia. "I've got half the county coming to watch."

Kat glanced at Harry. She knew that though Lavinia liked to make an old-fashioned fuss, she would probably be the first in line for a spin in the air if any of the pilots offered.

"Ah look – here's Benton!" said Harry. "He's wearing that 'something urgent' look."

Kat turned to see Lavinia's butler emerging from the house.

"Telephone call from London, sir," he said. "Miss Earhart has 'taken off', if that is the correct expression?"

"It is indeed," said Harry. "Got the windsock flying?"

"Yes, sir. And the gardener has also marked out the meadow precisely as you requested."

"Jolly good," said Harry. "Thought the old tennis court paint-roller would do the trick!"

"So – what do we do now?" said Kat.

"I suggest we organise a pot of coffee for our visitor, and then sit back and relax. She'll be here in no time."

Kat could tell Harry was excited about this. As was she.

"Just time to finalise lunch arrangements with Mrs Woodfine," Lavinia said and she walked off with Benton towards the house.

Kat meanwhile, squinting in the bright sunlight, peered into the sky to the north, so excited to finally be meeting the flying legend.

But as yet – there was not a sign.

NOW THAT SHE had the *Firefly* at a comfortable cruising altitude, Amelia began to *play with the plane*.

With a full tank, she knew she had plenty of time – and empty airspace – to have a little fun.

Weaving through dotted white clouds, she powered south, over the Sussex Downs, past woods and fields and tiny villages, until, within just minutes, she was crossing the coast.

She checked her map and peered out of the cockpit. To her right – that must be Portsmouth and the Isle of Wight. To port – Brighton.

She contemplated a low run along the beachfront, just for fun.

But no. Best use the time to rehearse.

For the weekend's big display – the finale to her fundraising trip – she had already built a planned repertoire of moves in her head, not shared with anyone, even O'Brien.

Didn't want anyone arguing against performing this or that manoeuvre.

She knew the *Firefly* handled the basic acrobatic tricks just fine. A barrel roll? Not a hitch. Loops, rolls and spins? The plane performed them all wonderfully. And when climbing into a big loop before going completely upside down, and then back to steady and level flight path? Perhaps one of the finest planes she had ever flown.

But there was one manoeuvre that she *hadn't* tried.

Though she imagined O'Brien or even Smythe might have guessed that – sooner or later – she would give it a shot.

She banked hard, heading inland again. Then she pulled back on the stick and eased open the throttle, pushing the nose of the plane up, climbing steadily, the air seeping in through the closed side windows now turning chilly.

Minutes later, with the altimeter showing ten thousand feet – the cars, houses and farm buildings below looking like such delicate miniatures, and the English Channel sparkling silver behind her – she levelled off.

She had read in Lindy's book *WE*, that he talked to himself when he crossed the Atlantic for the first time. Such a long flight – and only a stowaway housefly for company.

Amelia didn't usually do that. But now she felt like talking.

"Okay. Let's see how you do, girl."

Her *Firefly* suddenly anthropomorphised into a female of the species.

She checked her instruments.

All looking good. She gently dropped one wing and pushed the plane's nose down. Just a bit – altimeter already starting to spin in the other direction.

She pushed the plane into a full-on power dive. Though Amelia had performed this manoeuvre many times before, it was always exciting.

To aim this magical flying machine nearly straight down?

Then, to pull *out* of it?

Amazing.

She sharpened her downward angle, the front windshield now looking down at the lush woods and fields thousands of feet below, and her *Firefly* began to dive.

HARRY REACHED ACROSS the table to the plate of biscuits, offered it to Kat, then plucked his favourite, the one with the perfect little red circle of jam.

"All right, Lavinia's going to put you right next to Miss Earhart at the big dinner tomorrow night, you know."

"I feel honoured."

"And so you should," said Harry. "I'll probably be sandwiched between some old military buffers. I mean—"

But then Harry stopped.

He heard a buzzing.

A throaty sound he knew well.

An aeroplane engine.

"Oh!" said Kat, clearly hearing it too. "Is that her?"

He craned away from his wife, and looked up to the previously empty blue sky, and then to the south, where – high, so high – he saw a plane.

"Wrong direction," he said. "Must be one of the others."

He shielded his eyes from the sun: the distant plane – nose down, engine racing – was hurtling earthward at hundreds of miles an hour.

"Whoever it is," said Harry. "I hope they know what the hell they're doing."

AMELIA SAW THE land below, now *zooming* up to meet her.

The sound of the engine steady and reassuring, throttle eased, as gravity did the work, the engine ready to pull her out as needed.

But just when she felt that the plane had performed the manoeuvre in good form, Amelia heard a *cough*.

The engine *sputtered*. Once, then twice, until – the ground still looming – the propeller came to a full stop.

The noise replaced by the simple, shrill whistle of the air as she plummeted.

The engine had died.

A quick press to the ignition. *Nothing.*

A glance at the fuel gauge – both tanks still showing full. Amelia didn't permit herself to think exactly what that meant.

Instead, she slid open her side window, and looked down.

Every decision now needing to be made *fast*.

First things first – to get out of this dive.

She needed every foot of height she could steal – because height would give her time.

She pulled hard on the stick and felt the *Firefly* respond.

Good girl.

Slowly the nose lifted, then more. Amelia immediately saw that – straight ahead – thick woods awaited her, ready to rip the *Firefly* to pieces.

But to her left, she spotted a rolling field.

Not a neat, flat area – but at least no trees, no visible outcrops of rock. Maybe a place to land?

She turned into the wind, sacrificing more height.

So far, so good.

The field now directly ahead. To one side – a village. And, a mile or so north of that, a big country house.

At least she wasn't going to hit *that*.

Or so she hoped.

KAT LOOKED UP at the sky and saw what Harry had noticed.

"Oh no. The engine's dead," he said, staring up into the sky.

She came to her husband – who she knew had seen such things, of course, during the war. *Planes shot down – pilots trapped.*

A topic that Harry rarely discussed with her.

Now she could feel his tension, his fear.

"Is it going to clear the woods?" she said.

"Going to be tight," said Harry.

He started moving, running flat-out, racing over to where his BSA motorbike sat propped up by the side of the manor house.

She called, "Harry, what are you—?"

But the answer to that became clear as he hopped on the bike, gave it a quick kick-start, made a sharp, spinning turn, and headed straight out across the meadow.

"Got to see if I can help," he shouted over his shoulder.

She watched Harry disappear, spinning away. She turned to the distant plane.

It was too horrible to watch – yet she was unable to look away.

AMELIA HAD SURVIVED crashes before. She knew there really was only one rule in situations like this – keep your focus on responding to every move of the plane.

Don't think about what might happen.

In short, don't be afraid.

Fly the machine the best that you can.

She almost couldn't look ahead, even as the ground finally slipped lower on the windshields, with the plane still only just above the treacherous trees.

A glance at the turn coordinator showed she was level.

The moment so silent, with no rumbling engine, just the whistle of the wind.

The rolling open land ahead. *Close.*

She took a breath.

Time to land the Firefly.

HARRY CUT THROUGH a footpath, startling an old man smoking an elaborate pipe who was walking a collie. The man shook his head in total disapproval at a *motorbike* on a path made for pedestrians.

No matter, this would be the quickest way to where that plane was coming down.

Harry – while navigating the muddy trail, wheels slipping, the bike itself threatening to slide to the ground – risked a look ahead.

And what he saw was a damn fine piece of flying.

The plane had cleared Willis Woods. Beyond that lay farmland, open fields – a chance to land.

And live.

AMELIA FELT THE wheels hit the grassy land *hard*, and the plane bounced up as if stung, then down again.

With a sharp tilt, the left tyre hit an indentation in the ground.

For a second, she thought it might send the *Firefly* cartwheeling. And even at a slow speed, that would be a mess.

No guarantee of walking away from that one.

But another small hummock on the right actually helped her landing, righting the rolling plane.

Her speed slowed and, though the plane still jiggled and bumped, with the realisation that the danger was over, she actually laughed.

She was *okay*.

And so was the *Firefly*, as it hopped and bumped a few more feet to a stop.

4.

WELCOME TO SUSSEX

HARRY'S BIKE BOUNCED crazily over the field, but he could see that the pilot had brought the plane down safely, the machine bathed in the rich sunlight as if nothing untoward happened.

He kept the bike racing until he pulled up right beside the plane.

Off the bike, and onto the wing, propeller still. A powerful smell of aviation fuel stinging his nose. The cockpit closed.

Maybe the pilot was unconscious?

He opened the cockpit door, and started to pull the pilot out.

But the pilot turned – looked at him as if he had got off the wrong bus.

"Excuse me?"

"Best get you out of here, pal. Away from the plane. Make sure it's safe."

In response, the pilot pulled off their aviator cap and said, "Perfectly able to get out myself. Thank you."

And Harry realised.

That face known all around the world, especially with that disarming smile.

Eyes looking bold, the hair short, tousled. The freckled face.

No doubt. This was *Amelia Earhart.*

Harry leaned back as Amelia got up, and hopped past him to the ground.

He had been ready to upbraid the pilot for the crazy aerobatics.

But now, he could only say, "Bit of a close one there, Miss Earhart."

At that, Amelia looked back at the plane, still smiling Harry saw, as if unimpressed with very idea of a "close one".

"Yes, I know. Still, she did so well. Handled beautifully."

"Well, you *are* alive. Interesting landing."

"Sure was."

"Any idea what happened?"

The famous aviatrix turned back to him.

"No, Mr—"

"Harry. Er, sorry. Sir Harry Mortimer."

She nodded. "Lost power. Fuel line problem, I think."

Harry looked at the inside of the plane. Though he didn't fly much these days – and this plane was unfamiliar and new – the display of instruments all looked perfectly fine.

He jumped down from the cockpit.

"Just cut out, hmm?"

"Some kind of blockage," Amelia said, stepping back to look at the plane.

Harry shook his head.

"During the dive?"

"Ah – you saw that? Shame. I was having fun."

Harry watched as Amelia made a circuit of the downed plane, checking for damage.

"Doesn't look too bad, does she?" he said.

He joined her – pulling on struts, checking the undercarriage.

"You a flyer?" said Amelia, seeing him running his hands over the tips of the prop.

"Once upon a time," said Harry, and he saw Amelia registering him properly now.

And probably guessing just where he had got his flying experience.

"Pilot?"

"SE5s," he said, "among others."

Amelia nodded, then began looking around the great open field.

"Don't think you'll get her back in the air from here," said Harry.

"No, you're right."

Harry gestured to his bike: "Perhaps I can give you a lift?"

Amelia smiled at that. "That would be so very good of you. It's a place, not far I think, called Mydworth Manor. Know it?"

Harry grinned.

"Why, *yes I do*. It's my aunt's house."

"Ah," said Amelia. "That explains the 'Sir Harry' bit. My first knight of the realm. And rescuing a damsel in distress too. They all like you?"

"Ha, flyers with motorbikes? I think not."

She laughed. Then, she looked back at the plane.

"What about the *Firefly*?"

"Not to worry. I can make some calls. Shouldn't be a problem. I'll make sure she's safe."

Apparently reassured, she gave him a quick nod.

Harry walked over to his motorbike, flicked the stand and climbed on.

"Hop on. It'll be a bit of a bumpy ride back. But I rather imagine, after what you just did, you won't find it too *unsettling*."

Harry kick-started the engine and Amelia slipped behind him and held tight as he drove away from her plane, across the meadows that led to Mydworth Manor and his wife Kat.

KAT WATCHED AMELIA sip the tea. She actually looked shy – not at all what Kat had imagined.

"Cookie?" Kat said. "Our housekeeper Maggie baked them this morning. Quite tasty."

Amelia smiled, taking one of the shortbreads then – rather unexpectedly – dipping it into her milky tea.

"Very good," said Amelia. Then she gestured across the terrace to the Manor. "And your house, this kinda size too?"

Kat laughed at that. "Our old place? Not quite. Tad smaller – you'll have to drop by."

"Sounds like you've gotten used to this whole English aristocracy thing?"

"I wish," said Kat. "Got its own rules – and half the time they don't tell you what they are."

"Ah, yes. Guess the idea is to keep you on your toes, huh?"

"Maybe," said Kat, laughing. "Kinda growing to like it though."

Amelia looked around. "It is beautiful. The green, the trees, plants, it's…"

"I *know*. Pretty spectacular? Compensation for all the rain!"

Amelia laughed at that – cookie crumbs on her lip.

Kat, feeling already as if she had made a new friend, was enjoying these unexpected moments alone with the famous aviatrix.

"Lady Lavinia was so gracious, offering to host me, and the others coming with me. Then the air show over her property."

"Knowing Lady Lavinia, I think your Ninety-Nines are something she'd want to support all the way."

"Yes. And next year, a transcontinental race sponsored by the Ninety-Nines. Imagine – all female pilots from around the world! Just wish I'd been able to land on her field as planned."

Kat leaned over. "And *we're* just glad that that all turned out okay."

Amelia smiled. "Me too."

Which is when Kat saw Harry coming out of the French windows and across the terrace.

"O...*kay*," he said as he joined them. "I spoke to our good neighbour Barret just now on the telephone. Amelia, it's Mr Barret's field you landed in. He's organising a tractor to tow your plane over."

Kat saw Amelia nod. "Oh, that's great. I need my engineer to look at it as soon as possible."

"I've sent one of my aunt's men up to the plane to guard it," said Harry. "Young chap – chauffeur – very reliable. He won't let any harm come to her."

"Thank you."

"Oh, and about your engineer? And the other people coming along? Your sister, you say. You think they'll—"

But, as he spoke, Kat heard the sound of an approaching car.

They all looked across the terrace to the drive – where the most *yellow* of yellow Rolls-Royces was gliding towards the house.

"Well, speak of the devil," said Harry.

"Right," said Amelia putting down her tea and getting up. "I'd better go see them."

"Be right behind you," said Harry. "Oh – and in case my wife didn't warn you – brace yourself for the Byzantine world of an English country house. You may want to get back into that plane again."

"Oh, I always want to get back in that plane," said Amelia over her shoulder as she headed round to the front of the house, where the Rolls-Royce had pulled up.

Kat stood up.

"What do you say?" said Harry, softly. "About our guest?"

Kat stopped for a moment.

"I like her. And I have to say – she is one determined young woman."

"Agree," said Harry. "Add one thing to that."

"Yes?

"Add *brave*. That is one *brave* pilot."

5.

SABOTAGE

BY THE TIME Harry and Kat caught up with Amelia at the front of the house, greeting the occupants of the Rolls, Benton and other staff were unloading suitcases and bags.

Harry's first impression – *a bit of a flying circus.* Amelia – one arm around a young woman he guessed was her sister Pidge – made the introductions.

"Meet Pidge – my beloved sister – who does all the real work behind the scenes. Ronald Greene – reporter."

"Features writer, if you don't mind," said Greene with a slick smile, as he offered Harry and then Kat a brief handshake.

"Ronald takes my dull days, turns them into 'high adventure' for the world to read over breakfast," said Amelia. "Isn't that right, Ronald?"

"Oh, your adventures speak for themselves, dear Amelia. I am but the mouthpiece."

Something amiss between Amelia and the "features writer"? thought Harry. *She's making no effort to hide the fact she doesn't like him – and vice versa.*

Then he saw Amelia turn to a man in oil-stained overalls, who Harry instantly knew must be the engineer.

"Paddy O'Brien."

"Sir Harry," the man said, nodding to his oily hands. "Best we don't shake hands, sir."

"Quite understand," said Harry, smiling, but – yes – also catching a whiff of booze on the man's breath.

Hip flask somewhere hidden on his person, for sure.

"Finally, Mr Wallace Smythe, my agent for the trip."

Harry stepped forward and took in the man: bullish, with the air of a boxing promoter, braces stretched over a full shirt, a dicky bow askew under a wobbling chin, a valise clutched tightly under his arm.

"Pleased to meet you," said Smythe, then turned to Kat. "Lady Fitzhenry?"

"Actually, I'm Kat – Harry's wife," said Kat. "Lady Lavinia is in the house – she'll greet you all later, I'm sure."

As the servants carried the cases into the house, Harry saw O'Brien staring across towards the meadow, looking a little unsteady on his feet.

Confirming Harry's first whiff.

The man's been drinking already, Harry thought. *Not good at all.*

"So, then, where is the dear old kite?" said O'Brien. "Thought you had a landing field organised here?"

"Ah," said Amelia.

And she explained what had happened.

As she did, Harry watched her little entourage carefully: Pidge, eyes wide, clearly shocked by Amelia's lucky escape; O'Brien nervous, edgy; Greene excited, wanting details, notebook already out; and finally Smythe, surprisingly calm, evaluating.

All eyes were on Amelia – but for Harry, something was off. He couldn't figure what at first, then realised.

Nobody's asking questions about the stalled engine, the fuel problem.

There were no expressions of surprise. No alarm, no fear for Amelia and the plane. None.

Almost as if the near-fatal event hadn't come as a shock to any of them.

Only Pidge seemed to show any concern for Amelia.

"Now that's a story," said Greene, when Amelia finished. "Got any eye witnesses? Local farmer perhaps? Nanny out for a jaunt with a couple of terrified little ones?"

"None that I saw," said Harry. "Only me."

"I'd b-best get out there," said O'Brien. "Check the old girl over."

"I'll come with you," said Greene. "Grab some pictures while it's still light."

But some instinct made Harry step forward. "Sorry to disappoint you – afraid I've already arranged for her to be towed over."

"What?" said O'Brien.

"Better safe than sorry. Also – that field's miles away, take you forever by car. No good roads, just farm tracks."

"Really?" said Greene. "Bit of a damn shame."

"You sure, Sir Harry?" added Smythe. "Not much point having our own reporter if we can't capitalise on something like this, now is there?"

"The *Firefly* will be strapped to a trailer by now, I'm sure," said Harry. "Wasn't much to see anyway to be honest. Miss Earhart brought her down light as a feather. Not a scratch."

Harry saw Smythe and Greene share a quick look.

"Ah well, probably for the best," said O'Brien looking relieved. "Saves me humping all me tools cross country."

Harry waited while the three men hovered uncertainly for a moment, then they all seemed to agree to let it go.

Again – all of this somehow *odd*.

"Tell you gents what. Why don't you get settled into the house, take advantage of my aunt's hospitality, have a quiet dinner tonight?" said Harry.

"Great idea," said Amelia, putting her arm round her sister again. "Going to be plenty busy this weekend. And I for one could do with a hot bath!"

"Wait till you see my aunt's bathtubs. More like swimming pools!" said Harry, then turning to the rest. "So, everyone – just follow Benton there and he'll have one of the maids show you to your rooms."

"Er, where shall I be putting myself, sir?" said O'Brien.

For a moment Harry wished that Amelia's engineer would be with the rest. But England still being old England, *that was not to be.*

"Mr O'Brien, I believe there's a room been prepared for you above the stables over there," said Harry, pointing the way. "Also, got billets for ground crew. And you can stack your tools in the stable, horses have been moved out, of course."

"Will that be where they'll bring the *Firefly*?" said O'Brien, wiping at his lips.

"Believe so," said Harry.

As Benton led Amelia and Pidge away, Smythe took Harry to one side.

"Quick word, Sir Harry?" said Smythe.

Without waiting for an answer, he ushered Harry away and lowered his voice.

"Got a considerable sum of cash in here," he said, tapping his attaché case. "Takings from the last two weeks." He took a breath. "A lot."

"Cash? Is that wise?"

"Apparently the best way for Amelia to take the money back to the States for her project. Trouble with international cheques, so I'm told."

"I see," said Harry. "I imagine you'd like me to put it in Benton's house safe?"

"I'll do it," said Smythe brusquely. "Just have your fellow assist me."

"Of course. Just follow Benton and he'll look after you."

"Appreciate it. Can't be too careful *these* days." Then he turned to Greene: "Tell you what – Greene, why don't you accompany me, extra pair of eyes and what not."

"Happy to," said Greene, slinging a camera case over his shoulder, and joining Smythe.

Harry nodded at that, and waited while Smythe and Greene hurried after Benton, and O'Brien climbed in the Rolls and drove off towards the stables.

Then he turned to Kat.

"Well, what do you make of that? Seemed – I don't know – a tad odd."

"I agree. And the weekend's hardly even started!"

"In fact," said Harry. "Apart from the delightfully named Pidge—"

"What's that? Short for pigeon?"

"One can only guess," said Harry. "But apart from her, nobody seemed terribly bothered that she ran out of fuel and nearly crashed."

"You're right," said Kat. "I mean – the engineer, O'Brien – shouldn't he be all over it, wanting details, times, the works?"

"Sadly, I think our Mr O'Brien has more interest in the hip flask he has secreted in the top pocket of those overalls."

"Yes. I noticed that he seemed a bit wobbly. But this is terrible, Harry, isn't it? I mean – Amelia, with these clueless people around her… That engineer… She could be in real danger."

"Yes, and that is why you and I are going to hop on the old bike and check out the *Firefly*."

"I thought you said it had already been moved?"

"You didn't believe me, did you? Oh, I am *good*. Just wanted them to think the plane was already in transit. No – we need to look it over with no one the wiser."

"You're not suggesting this was more than just an accident?"

"Good Lord, no. Sloppy maintenance, more like. But in the flying business that can be fatal."

"The others didn't seem too concerned."

"They should be," said Harry. "I certainly am."

Then Kat gestured to the bike. "Come on then. Let's get to work."

Harry watched as she walked over to the bike, flicked the stand with her foot and kicked the engine into life.

She nodded to the back of the bike. "You get the – let's call it – liar's seat," she said.

"Not sure I like the ring of *that*," said Harry.

But then, grinning, he climbed aboard behind her, and slipped his arms around her waist.

"Steady, tiger," she said, as with a roar of the engine, they hurtled away towards the meadow.

KAT TOOK THE fields and the narrow footpath carefully. With two of them on the big BSA, navigation wasn't easy as the rutted ground pulled the machine from side to side, threatening to send them flying.

But finally she crested a rise to look down and see the already famous *Firefly*, so incongruous, sitting bang in the middle of this field above Mydworth.

Squatting on the wing in the soft evening sunshine, she recognised Huntley, Lavinia's young undergardener and chauffeur from the manor.

To one side, loosely roped to a tree, Kat recognised one of Lavinia's mares, a big solid workhorse.

"Sir Harry, m'lady," he said, jumping up as she brought the bike right up to the plane and she and Harry climbed off. "Rode up soon as Benton brought me your message, sir."

"Good man, Huntley," said Harry, patting him on the shoulder. "We had any visitors?"

"Mr Barret came up, took one look, went back for his big trailer and some of his lads. Think he'll winch her up, take her by road."

"Makes sense," said Kat, walking over to the plane, thinking how smooth, how beautiful the lines, how simple the layout, like a sports car.

Maybe time I took up flying, she thought. *One thing, this sleek aircraft is nothing like the old biplanes. The future of flight for sure.*

"I'm guessing you never flew anything at all like this?" she said to Harry.

"Isn't she a beauty?" he said. "Back in the day, my squadron would have given their eye teeth—"

"Well, you know what?" said Kat, turning and smiling, "Carry on being nice to our new friend, maybe she'll give you a ride."

"Well, maybe she will," said Harry, coming closer, holding her gaze and smiling mischievously.

She knew he could read her expression: *Better watch your step, Sir Harry.*

"Fuel tanks?" said Kat, spinning away.

He laughed.

"Where are they?" she said.

Harry pointed behind the pilot's seat and up into the wings.

"I imagine for the trip this morning though, they only filled the main tank, and the reserve," he said.

"You think Amelia's right? It was just a blockage in one of the pipes?" she said.

"That might explain things," said Harry. "Especially from the way she described it. But…"

"But?"

"I don't know. The more I think about it, the more I sense there's something fishy about all this."

She watched him go back to the bike, open the small tool box over the back wheel and take out a flashlight.

"Let's check the fuel, the lines, ourselves, shall we?" he said, returning to the plane.

He crouched down next to the fuselage and unscrewed a cap with a small chain on it, then when it was loose, clicked the flashlight on and pointed it into the hole.

"Well, there's a thing," he said. "Take a look."

Kat crouched next to him, adjusted the flashlight, peered in.

"Can't see anything."

"Exactly. Tank's empty."

He put the cap back on then they both stood up.

"Perhaps she got a leak?"

Harry nodded to the grass under the plane. "Few oil drips. No sign of any fuel."

"So maybe they didn't put enough gas in back in London?"

"Fuel gauges full on take-off, she said."

"Only one way to find out," said Kat, climbing up onto the wing and sliding into the cockpit.

Secretly thrilled to be sitting where Amelia Earhart plied her trade.

Harry climbed up on the wing next to her and peered into the cockpit over her shoulder.

"You understand all this? The dials, levers?" said Kat.

"Pretty much. Hasn't really changed much since my day."

"Fuel gauges?" she said, pointing to four dials to her left, needles on a half clockface.

"That's right," said Harry. "Bottom two are long-range, I imagine – both on empty."

"Top two – on full, like she said."

"Ah well," said Harry. "That's interesting. Damned interesting."

"Oh? Why?"

"Because with the power off – they should be reading empty."

"What?"

"Electrical gauges," said Harry, "just like on the Alvis. They only work when you turn the ignition on."

"Wait a second," said Kat. "You saying that they – somehow – became jammed?"

Kat didn't wait for his answer, and instead pressed as close as she could to the dials.

Close enough to see… a small pin.

A needle inserted through the back of the dial, holding the indicator against the word "FULL".

She sat back, then looked up at Harry, leaning against the side of the cockpit.

"They *didn't* jam, Harry," she said. "They *were* jammed."

"What?"

"Look. Someone's fixed the gauge so it reads full – and stays that way."

"Whether or not she had fuel in the tank," said Harry. "Good God. That doesn't make any sense. Why? Crazy."

"It is. But Harry – not just crazy. Surely – attempted murder?"

And Harry's grim silence was enough of an answer.

6.

SUSPICIONS

HARRY DIPPED A toasted "soldier" into his boiled egg, and lifted another newspaper from the pile on the Dower House breakfast table.

"Oh – this one's even better," he said, as Kat, in her silk dressing gown, brought more toast to the table and poured another coffee. "Listen: *'Brave Amelia wrestled with the controls of the runaway fighter plane, using all her skills and feminine wiles to avoid the crowded Mydworth School playground'.*"

"Playground? She wasn't anywhere near. Let me guess: Ronald Greene again?"

"The very man. Six front pages he's bagged so far. And how the hell he got up there in time to take a photo I do not know."

"Masculine wiles?" said Kat. "They do top everything, don't they?'

"Don't ask me," said Harry, brushing toast crumbs from his pyjamas. "Think I lost my 'wiles' years ago. Late night in Berlin, I believe."

"Was I there, darling?"

"Wish you had been," said Harry, giving her a wink as he sipped his tea.

"I had Maggie pick up all the dailies," said Kat. "But there's one in particular you should see."

Harry watched her leaf through the pile, then pick up the most lurid of the news-sheets, and fold it open.

The centre-spread photo: a picture of the *Firefly* being towed on a trailer through Mydworth, surrounded by a crowd of waving bystanders.

"See who's standing up on the trailer?" said Kat.

Harry looked carefully and there was Wallace Smythe, proudly holding a wing strut, posing for the camera.

"And the credit on the photo?" said Kat.

Harry glanced at the caption: *Amelia's brave Firefly feted by Sussex villagers. Photo: Ronald Greene.*

"So much for keeping people away from the plane," said Harry.

"Greene must have made hundreds from those exclusives."

"Wonder if Amelia sees a penny? I doubt it."

"So what are we going to do?" said Kat. "The plane sabotaged. Do we have a plan? I seem to remember last night we decided to sleep on it?"

"We did. Not that I've got any more answers this morning. You?"

"Nope. Is it possible there's an innocent explanation?"

"For rigging a plane's fuel gauge?" said Harry. "Can't for the life of me think of one."

"Me neither," said Kat. "My instinct says we talk to the mechanic first. Then go from there?"

"We can get him early. When he's still sober," said Harry reaching for the marmalade and more toast. "Should we tell Amelia what we know?"

He saw Kat turn away, thinking on the question. A slight chew of her lower lip.

"Okay. I'm thinking *not yet*. Unless she's planning on taking the *Firefly* up again today – in which case, we don't have a choice."

"Agree," said Harry.

"What time are the other planes arriving at the manor?" said Kat.

But both of them stopped, and looked up to the ceiling as a plane roared low over the house, the noise making dogs in the town bark and howl.

"Ah," said Kat.

"Head up there in ten?" said Harry.

"Twenty," said Kat, and he watched her go upstairs to dress.

Just time for one more slice, he thought, reaching for the toast. *I have a feeling it's going to be a long day.*

HARRY PULLED THE Alvis in a wide curve past the fountain at the front of Mydworth Manor – then round the side of the house to the stables – the place already a hive of activity.

He could see two, no, three biplanes already parked up in a line, crew and pilots working, inspecting, chatting together.

And to one side – the *Firefly*, now looking as if yesterday had never happened.

On the far meadow, a refuelling area had been set up, as he'd specified, with a couple of bowsers, portable fuel tanks, already in place.

And the whole paved area in front of the stables – where usually the horses would be groomed and walked – was now an impromptu workshop, with benches stacked with tools and spare plane parts.

Quite the scene.

"There's O'Brien," said Kat, as he turned off the engine.

Harry saw the mechanic emerge from underneath the fuselage of the *Firefly*, swap spanners from a toolbox, then roll back under the plane.

He climbed out of the car, then turned to Kat.

"Tell you what," he said. "Why don't I see what I can get out of him, while you check who's up and about in the house?"

"Sounds good to me," said Kat. "After that little photo display, Mr Greene has some explaining to do."

"Play nicely now, darling."

"Oh, I will," said Kat, unpinning her hair after the drive in the car. "He'll hardly know he's been mauled."

Harry laughed as she shook her hair loose, then he watched her turn and walk back towards the house.

That bright yellow dress – *cheap old thing as she called it.* On Kat? She looked like a million dollars.

"MR O'BRIEN?" said Harry, leaning down to peer underneath the *Firefly*, where the mechanic was tightening a bolt on the tail skid.

"What is it?" said O'Brien, not looking up. "Can't you see I'm busy, for – oh, Sir Harry, that you? Give me a couple of minutes, sir."

"No problem. Mind if I take a tour of the cockpit?"

"Fill your boots."

Harry stepped up onto the wing – then eased himself over and into the seat.

This cockpit, in some ways so familiar – all the dials, the leather, the smell – but so much was new.

Not surprising. It was more than ten years since he'd flown regularly, patrolling the deadly skies over France and Belgium.

He pushed those thoughts away, and leaned forward to check the fuel gauges.

All of them now standing at EMPTY.

Not a sign of the tiny pins that had held those need indicators on FULL.

So somebody had slipped back into the cockpit and removed the evidence.

But who? And an even bigger question: *why?*

It wasn't going to be easy to find out: it was clear from Greene's newspaper photos that people had been crawling all over the *Firefly*.

And, even now, back here at the manor house, the plane was hardly under lock and key.

Harry looked out from the cockpit, across the flat meadow where another biplane was just touching down, and thought back to the strange reactions of Amelia's team when they'd arrived yesterday.

Unlikely as it seemed – could the suspect even be one of them?

Greene the journalist? Or Smythe? Both of whom had clearly spent time near the plane yesterday.

Though he could hardly imagine Smythe had the frame to squat inside the cockpit and fix the gauges.

But what could possibly be the motivation for any of them doing that?

"There. I'm all yours, sir," said O'Brien and Harry looked round to see the mechanic roll out from under the plane and draw himself slowly up.

Harry climbed out of the cockpit and hopped down onto the grass.

He shook O'Brien's hand, the man wiping his hands on his overalls first.

Those overalls: tightly buttoned, even though it was already a warm morning. O'Brien's face glazed with sweat.

"Sorry, sir, got a lot of checks to do on her, people keep coming over wanting the full tour."

"Not surprising – she's one heck of a machine. A real beauty. You're a lucky man getting to work on her."

"I am indeed, sir, I am indeed," said O'Brien.

Harry leaned back against the side of the *Firefly*, shining in the morning sun.

"You work for Sandbourne, yes?"

"Ah, no sir. Mr Smythe – he hired me especially for the tour."

"Really? Imagine it must have taken a while to learn the ropes – new machine like this?"

"Twenty years I've worked on planes, sir. I know what I'm doing."

"Oh, I'm sure you do," said Harry. "You served, I imagine?"

Harry dropped the question lightly, expecting O'Brien to start the usual exchange of wartime postings, places, people.

But instead, the engineer just nodded and offered nothing more.

Harry paused, then smiled. For many, those wartime years were best forgotten – and he respected that.

"Long time ago, eh?" he said.

"Indeed, sir," said O'Brien. "Now, er, how can I be helping you?"

"Oh, I won't take up too much of your time, old chap, just want to be absolutely sure there won't be any more *mishaps* while Miss Earhart is our guest."

"The landing? Ah yes, right."

"You've seen Miss Earhart this morning?"

"Came over first thing, sir. Desperate to go up, she was. But I said that wasn't possible."

"Plane damaged?"

"Far as I can tell, sir? No. But I want the whole day to test every inch. Better safe than sorry."

"So no flying for the lady today, eh?"

"She gave me a bit of an argument, but that's right, sir. I've got the day to make sure all is as it should be. Safe and sound!"

Harry watched him carefully. The man was nervous, twitchy even. But Harry knew the morning nerves might just be the alcohol.

Bad hangover will do that to you.

"But you found the fuel blockage, I imagine?"

"Blockage, sir?"

"Yes, you see Miss Earhart said yesterday she had a full tank of fuel when she took off, but somehow the flow to the engine stopped."

Harry smiled, scratched his head as if understanding the technicalities might be beyond him.

While in fact he well understood how such things were supposed to work.

"Yes, forgive me if I'm not interpreting those facts correctly, O'Brien, but that would suggest a pipeline blockage, no?"

"Well, yes, sir – it would. But—but—"

The mechanic seemed to have stuttered to a halt.

"Yes?" Harry said, doing his best to keep what he hoped was a disarming smile on his face.

While thinking: *Come on man, out with it.*

"Sir, what you say, makes sense. But I've not seen any sign of such a thing. So... I don't know what to say. I—I—"

The man's eyes now wide – the look of someone feeling suddenly *cornered.*

Harry realised he was going to have to take a new tack.

He took a step closer and let his smile fade.

O'Brien took notice, eyes fixed on Harry's.

"Listen to me, O'Brien" he said, quietly. "Things happen, yes? But if you think there's a problem I should know about, you'd best tell me right now."

Harry took a breath, letting his words sink in.

"You've a pilot's life in your hands. And, in this case, not just *any* pilot, right? And what you're feeling now is nothing compared to how you'll feel if any harm comes to Miss Earhart."

Funny, Harry thought. He'd told Kat to go easy with her questioning. While Harry had instinctively decided to do *just the opposite.*

O'Brien licked at his lips, another nervous *tic.* The man looked about as guilty as he could.

Then, hoping to soften things a bit, Harry said, "I promise you, if you know anything, it won't go any further."

Harry waited, watching this sink in. Then, like a dam breaking, O'Brien spoke: "Sir, here's the thing. Appreciate what you're saying, I do! But what happened to Amelia? I *can't* explain it. Can't fathom it at all."

"What do you mean? You can't find any blockage?"

"There *was* no blockage. Lines working just fine. There just wasn't any fuel."

"What on earth do you mean?" said Harry, pretending to be surprised.

"Back at the aerodrome, they signed off a full tank, fuelled up, all ready to go. And the gauges – well they were playing up a bit, but, you know, the *Firefly* – she's still a prototype, you expect glitches. Anyway, last minute, before Miss Earhart took off, I powered her up, and checked the cockpit gauges – they said the tank was *full*."

Harry watched O'Brien take out his oil rag, wipe the sweat from his face, leaving a tell-tale smudge on his brow before he tucked it back in his top pocket.

"But – you see, sir – turns out – the tank *wasn't* full at all. It must have been nearly empty. And the reserve – well that can't have been more than fumes."

"Good God, O'Brien!" he said. "But wait – didn't you do a manual check of the tanks too?"

Harry knew this should have been usual procedure. He watched O'Brien carefully, the man wringing the oily cloth in his hands again, in discomfort.

"I would have done, normally sir, course I would. But what with all the fuss going on, the BBC, the cameras…"

A likely story, thought Harry. *You were half-cut already, pal, and that's why you look so damn guilty.*

DANGER IN THE AIR

Harry waited, thinking this through. He hadn't mentioned the fixed fuel gauges yet. And he decided not to.

Because O'Brien, as wobbly as he was, seemed to be genuinely in the dark about what had happened and perhaps even ashamed he'd not done his job properly.

Harry knew that, if he was right, then back at the aerodrome someone had deliberately only put *half* a tank on board.

And that meant there was a conspiracy at work here.

A conspiracy to kill Amelia Earhart.

But why on earth?

He took a deep breath. "*Righto*. Why don't we start from the beginning? Tell me how you got this job, and exactly — moment by moment — what happened at the aerodrome yesterday morning."

KAT WALKED DOWN the long hallway of Mydworth Manor, nodding to the stream of servants busily heading to and from the dining room and the ballroom.

The staff were working flat-out to prepare for tonight's cocktails and dinner — then the lunch party tomorrow to accompany the aerial display.

She spotted Benton.

"Everybody down already, Benton?" she said.

"Lady Lavinia has taken breakfast in her room, m'lady," said Benton. "And I believe Miss Earhart and Mr Smythe are having a private meeting in the library."

"Any sign of Mr Greene?"

"The *reporter*, m'lady?"

Kat always found Benton to be the sturdiest of supporters of the English class system, his disdain for the — in his mind — *dubious* profession of journalism quite clear from his tone.

"That's the guy."

"As far as I know, he is taking coffee with Miss Earhart's sister in the drawing room."

"Ah, thanks. I'll join them."

"In which case, I shall have coffee brought to you," said Benton, and with a nod he turned on his heels.

Kat went to the library. The door was shut.

She tapped and went in.

On the sofa under the window sat Greene and Amelia's sister, Pidge. Kat sensed that had she come in a minute earlier she might have found them sitting a damn sight closer to each other.

"Morning," she said. "Mind if I join you two for coffee?"

"Not at all," said Greene. "I'm just educating Miss Earhart here on the pros and cons of the English aristocracy."

I bet you were, thought Kat.

"Lords, earls, barons, dukes, knights," said Pidge. "The whole deal's way too complicated – my head's spinning!"

Kat laughed. "Oh, I still say the wrong thing all the time, and I'm supposed to be one of 'them'!" she said, taking the armchair next to them. "I think my gaffes in that area have become quite the comedic entertainment at dinner parties."

She watched Greene take out a cigarette from a silver case and light up.

"Mr Greene, I saw your work in the papers this morning," said Kat. "Amazing luck, you chancing upon the plane heading through the town."

"Wasn't it?" said Greene, his face a smug challenge. "Wallace and I had just popped down there for a snifter before dinner."

"Must be quite a payday, all those front pages?"

"I suppose it is," said Greene with a shrug. "But it's my job to get Amelia and the plane right into the public eye."

"Of course. I guess, in a funny way, her plucky escape helps you to do just that? Quite the show to write about."

"You know, it wasn't a 'show' and it wasn't funny," said Pidge – and Kat realised that having the younger sister here was going to make the interview tricky.

"No, not funny, you're right," Kat said quickly. "Awful choice of words! Terrifying, I imagine."

"True," said Greene. "But though Amelia's a fine pilot, just being an amazing aviatrix isn't enough of a story. So, to be honest – sorry, Pidge – when something goes a little *awry* well, it gives our whole 'show' a boost."

Does it indeed? thought Kat. *Gives Greene's bank balance a boost too, I bet.*

"Like the high-wire performer in the circus?" she said, her eyes now locked on Greene's.

"Gosh I hope not!" said Pidge. "Terrible things can happen to them! I worry enough about my sister."

But neither Kat nor Greene glanced at her – Kat could sense Greene got where she was coming from now.

"You know, they say the high-wire act is actually the *safest* one in the show," said Greene, taking a long draw on his cigarette then tapping the ash into the tray on the coffee table.

"That why you weren't worried about Amelia's crash-landing yesterday?"

Greene laughed.

"Short of a wing coming off, I can't imagine anything happening up there that that girl couldn't deal with."

"Ronald!" said Pidge, giving him a playful punch on the arm. "You mustn't talk like that! A wing coming off – heaven forbid!" Pidge took a deep breath. "Can we please talk about something else!"

"Sorry, my dear," said Greene. "You know I'd do anything for your sister. I *adore* her."

At which point a maid arrived with Kat's coffee.

Kat looked at Greene, deciding for now there wasn't much more she could ask.

Not with Pidge there, getting upset.

Did he really 'adore' Amelia? she wondered.

Or did he adore the dollars flowing in her wake?

In which case: how far would he go to keep those dollars flowing?

7.

WHERE'S AMELIA?

HARRY STOOD ON the front steps of the manor house with Kat, watching an old Sopwith Pup take off from the improvised landing strip.

It was a perfect morning for flying: wisps of high cloud, the sky a soft blue, and hardly a breeze fluttering the improvised windsock out in the meadows.

He smiled as the Sopwith's nose lifted almost nervously, as if unsure about the whole absurd *notion* of flight, then – as the pilot committed and the revs rose – suddenly pinged confidently into the air, climbing fast.

"That the kind of thing you used to fly?" said Kat.

He shaded his eyes as the tiny biplane jostled into the sky.

"To start with," he said.

"You'll have to teach me one day."

"What? So you can be better than me at that too?"

"Just the natural order of things to come, darling," said Kat. "You'll get used to it one day."

"Not sure I like the sound of this 'future' you conjure up. But I'll tell you this, Lady Mortimer. From what I know of you? You'd absolutely *love* to fly one."

Then he looked over at the *Firefly*, parked on the rise by the stables, and next to him Kat followed his gaze.

"You think O'Brien was lying?" she said.

"Hard to tell – he's got the shakes so much. I asked him in detail about how they fuelled up at the aerodrome; he couldn't explain what had happened. You know, I must say he seemed genuinely mystified."

"Surely only the plane's mechanic would know how to tamper with the gauges, though?"

"Not necessarily," said Harry. "But anyway – that whole empty tank business. I've phoned a pal up at Great Western – he's going to have a sniff around. Check the invoices, fuel records. Anything amiss."

"Someone must have signed and paid for the fuel."

"Exactly."

"What if it's just a fuel scam that went wrong?" said Kat. "A few more minutes, and Amelia would have landed fine, no one the wiser?"

"So why the fixed gauges?"

"Part of the scam, perhaps?" said Kat.

"But then we come back to the question: who removed the pins?" said Harry. "The evidence vanishing. And would they really come all the way from West London overnight to cover their tracks?"

"True," said Kat. "Which suggests… should we be looking closer to home for the saboteur?"

"Saboteur? Interesting choice of word. And on Amelia's team?" said Harry, turning to her. "They all certainly behaved oddly yesterday – but, here's the thing, I can't figure a motive for harming Amelia, can you?"

"No. In fact, the opposite seems true."

"Go on."

"Well, take Greene for instance," said Kat. "No love lost between him and Amelia, granted. But, like I said, he's clearly making a fortune from every photo."

"You think he could have 'fixed' the plane for the publicity? He certainly lapped up the opportunity."

"That he did," said Kat. "But – okay – why would he risk killing the golden goose? This weekend is going to provide him with plenty more front pages, for sure."

"Right. Same with Smythe. Lavinia tells me he's making tons from this tour. In fact, Benton told me – *in confidence of course* – that Smythe's attaché case was absolutely *stuffed* with loot when he popped it in the house safe."

"And that's not even counting the donations your aunt's pals are bound to make to Amelia's cause this weekend," said Kat.

"Exactly."

"Which leaves – sorry, bit of a stretch here – Pidge," said Kat. "But she was the only one to show real shock at the news yesterday. And she jumped on Greene when he made light of it. All my instincts tell me that was completely genuine."

"Yup. And I can't really see Pidge fiddling with fuel gauges. Anyway, your 'instincts' – as we both know – are beyond question."

"Correct answer, Sir Harry."

"So, that brings us back to O'Brien," said Harry. "But, why would he risk his career on a stunt like that? I know plenty of engineers would give their eye teeth to work on a plane like the *Firefly*."

He waited as a small group of Lavinia's guests strolled across the gravel towards the stables.

Putting his hand up to shade his eyes, he saw the Sopwith, high in the sky, perform a perfect roll.

"Is the *Firefly* that special, Harry?" said Kat.

"Oh yes. Sandbourne Aviation have been lobbying the Ministry all year to give them a contract, put her straight into production. She's a world-beater."

"A lot of money at stake?"

Harry turned to look at his wife.

"Could say that. *Millions*," he said. And then he realised what Kat was suggesting. "Ah. I got you. *You* think maybe the target's not Amelia – but the plane itself?"

"I imagine Sandbourne aren't the only game in town?" said Kat.

"Indeed not. Plane design these days – it's a high stakes game. Very lucrative. Just guessing here, but Albion Aero for one," he said. "They've got a nifty little single-seater in play, called the *Bulldog*."

"Right! Isn't that one of the planes in the display tomorrow?"

"I do believe it is," said Harry.

"Bit of a coincidence that, don't you think?" said Kat. "The two planes, on show, side by side?"

"Indeed. And, now you mention it, I heard a few rumours around Whitehall that Albion's relations with Sandbourne recently hadn't been quite as *gentlemanly* as one might have wished."

"Could that stretch to sabotage?" said Kat.

"Aha, well that's one of the many big questions, detective! 'Fraid, as of now, we don't know much of anything, do we?"

He took her arm.

"Not that we haven't been there before, eh?" he said. "Come on. It's nearly lunchtime. Think it's all set on the side lawn. Let's grab some soup, check out the planes and pilots, and on the way you can tell me more about our friend Mr Greene."

KAT WATCHED HARRY pick up a neat triangle of a watercress and egg sandwich, crusts banished, and then take a large bite as if they were at Yankee Stadium, hot dog in hand between innings.

Behind him stretched a long table arranged with an assortment of tidy sandwiches, plates of cold meats, poached salmon and large tureens of soup.

A couple of young servants stood ready to serve, buffet style.

"Harry," she said. "Your aunt's certainly gone to great pains. I mean, this little lunch is not quite so *little*."

"Oh, in truth that's the work of good old Mrs Woodfine and company," said Harry, taking another large bite. "Aunt Lavinia's just in charge of giving the orders."

"Take it you are no fan of garden parties?"

"That what this is? Remind me never to throw one at the Dower House. And *that* reminds me, wherever *is* the champagne?"

"Think maybe with pilots flying today," Kat said, taking a sandwich herself, "that the bubbly was deemed a tad inappropriate."

She knew he was enjoying her reaction to his obvious display of non-gentility.

"If I told you how many times I took a sip of brandy before hitting the skies above our trenches... Don't know about other pilots, but it certainly helped me to keep a steady hand on the old stick, especially with a Fokker hot on my tail."

She saw him look around. Lavinia had said lunch would be an informal affair – pilots and other guests fitting in around preparations for the display tomorrow.

The only other guests here – so far – were Ronald Greene and Pidge, sitting together at one of the small picnic tables.

"So, this Greene fellow," said Harry, reaching across for a slice of meat pie. "He does seem rather glued to Amelia's sister."

"Yes. I don't think Amelia likes it one bit."

Harry nodded. "And, Lady Mortimer, your little chat with him? Any other useful observations?"

Kat leaned closer. "I can tell you this. Greene, with all those newspaper covers—"

"The lurid tales of Amelia's narrow escape from death?"

"Yes. Well, certainly no regrets on his part for playing up the story."

"Imagine a type like him would call it simply embellishment. Anything else occur to you?"

"He more or less acknowledged that those stories generated a good amount of money."

"And I take it Mr Greene likes money?" said Harry, his smile fading away as he wiped his mouth with a starched napkin.

"Oh yes. Makes no bones about it either."

Kat saw one of Benton's staff emerge from the house with a plate of sandwiches at the ready, almost held as if he was a liveried knight, ready to do battle.

Harry gave him a quick wave, stopping him in his tracks, and diverting the tray in their direction.

Kat waited for the sandwiches to be replenished, then when the servant had gone, leaned forward: "Joking aside, Harry, I am worried."

"About Amelia's safety?" said Harry.

"Yes," said Kat, taking some of the tiny cream cheese and cucumber squares and trying one. "But I've also been thinking, best we keep what we know to ourselves. For now."

"Agree. We'll have to tell her soon though."

"Course. Let's pick a good time, good place. We also really need to speak to Smythe. See if he knows anything about Albion Aero, perhaps."

"*And* if he saw anything untoward at Great Western Aerodrome."

"I would have thought he'd be out here, no?" said Kat.

"Guess so," said Harry. "Pilots about to do some practice runs in a bit. He is the promoter of the whole thing."

Harry looked around some more.

"And where *is* Amelia?"

A quick look told Kat that her fellow American wasn't out here. But then, down by the stables, where lunch had also been set out for the crews, she finally spotted her.

"Ah, down there. With the other pilots. Looks like she's coming up now."

And Kat watched as Amelia hurried up the gentle rise from the flat meadow that had been laid out as a runway, now dotted with a half dozen planes.

8.

YET ANOTHER WORRY

AMELIA CAME RUNNING up to them, a big smile on her face, wisps of hair blowing in the gentle wind.

"Amelia, been swapping tales with your fellow flyers?" said Kat.

"Yes! They're great. Tons of experience." Now Amelia leaned closer to the two of them. "And not at all stuffy around a female pilot. Could tell you – some of the chilly reactions I've had back in the States."

Kat smiled. "*That* I can believe. Run into some of that myself."

Harry pursed his lips. "Imagine you're rather disappointed you won't be flying this afternoon?"

But Kat saw Amelia's smile only broaden.

"Oh, no – but I *am* flying."

Now it was Kat's turn to look – in earnest – quite concerned. Instinctively her hand went to Amelia's right forearm.

"But Amelia, your plane. Still being checked out, isn't it?"

"No, not the *Firefly*. I want her checked properly, of course. But this pilot – a very nice Mr Tyler – said I can take up his de Havilland. Give her a spin. Go through my routine. I think – he's actually pleased I'll be flying it!"

Kat took a breath. Clearly the young woman standing there in front of her, grinning, didn't get to be a world-famous pilot by doing exactly what people told her.

"Oh, that's great then," said Kat.

"Isn't it."

Kat saw Amelia glance across at Ronald Greene and Pidge, still chatting together over lunch.

Bit of a frown there.

"I need to change. Something more suited for flying," Amelia said, turning from them, and literally running past Benton and his staff, into Mydworth Manor.

"Well, that's good to hear," Harry said, turning back to Kat. "I was rather afraid she'd go up in the *Firefly*, despite things."

"Me too," said Kat, getting up from the table. "Harry, I don't see Smythe here. Let's ask Benton if he knows where we can find him."

"Oh, Benton will know," said Harry, standing too. "That man knows *everything*, least as far as my aunt's property and guests goes."

Harry led the way to Benton who, seeing them, quickly proffered: "M'lady, Sir Harry."

"Benton, we were just wondering. Mr Smythe – has he already taken lunch? Or—"

Benton cleared his throat with what to Kat sounded like a head butler's grumble of disapproval.

"Er, no, Sir Harry. He's been on the house telephone for *quite* some time now. I imagine he is still talking."

Benton had kept his choice of words moderate.

But it was easy to hear from his tone how he felt about such monopolising of the manor house phone.

"Oh, thank you, Benton. Lady Mortimer and I just need a quick word with the man."

"Of course, sir."

And as Benton went back to surveying his staff, Harry gave Kat a quick smile, and led the way into the house. Where, only steps past the doorway, Kat could hear one very loud Wallace Smythe.

So loud! Does he actually need a phone to be heard? she wondered.

HARRY WALKED DOWN the hallway to the small table outside Lavinia's private sitting room. Said table held the house phone – and also a small lattice-backed chair.

But Mr Smythe was carrying on his conversation standing up, his back to Harry and Kat as they walked straight to him.

Hearing it all.

"I don't care *what* they said, now do I? You tell them that everything—" Then Smythe, caught in the maelstrom of his own tirade, finally became aware that two people stood close to him, awaiting his attention. Smythe seemed to forget himself. "Yes, *yes*. What is—" Then as if finally remembering exactly whose house this was, he put a hand over the mouthpiece of the phone and spoke more politely. "Sir Harry. Is there any—?"

Harry looked at Kat.

He guessed that Smythe would be one of those men who expected that the men did all the talking.

Kat, though, didn't miss a beat.

"Why yes there is, Mr Smythe. Think we could have a few words?"

Smythe's eyes darted from Harry, then to Kat. "What? Right now? You see—"

Harry grinned. "Would appreciate it awfully. Don't want to miss the little warm-up display outside in a bit, now do we?"

Cornered, Smythe removed his hand from the mouthpiece.

"I—I'll have to get back to you. Just don't go anywhere. Bye!"

And with a heavy click, he placed the now-liberated phone back on the small table.

"Now – what is it you need to so urgently talk to me about?"

"It's about Amelia, Mr Smythe, and what happened yesterday."

Harry had his eyes locked on the man. Did he expect this surprise interrogation?

Possibly, though he did look genuinely flummoxed.

"The unorthodox landing, you mean?" he said.

"Hardly the word I'd use," said Harry. "In fact, we're a little concerned that nobody seems to know exactly *what* happened."

"Ah, I see. Well, we're *all* concerned, aren't we? But all's well that ends—"

"Yes," Kat said. "That is, of course, if it has ended?"

"What on earth do you mean – not ended?" said Smythe.

Harry glanced at Kat, who looked ready to answer.

"You understand that Miss Earhart is a guest here at Mydworth, yes?" said Kat. "So, we feel a particular responsibility on behalf of Lady Lavinia to ensure her stay is a totally *safe* one."

At that moment, one of the maids appeared from the servery, carrying a tray of sandwiches – and all three of them paused until she had passed.

"Safe?" said Smythe. "What do you mean? Who says it's *not* safe?"

"Perhaps we might continue this conversation somewhere a little more private?" said Harry.

"Very well, then. If we must. Where shall we talk?"

Harry pointed to a hallway leading to the rear area of the manor house. "Let's pop out to the sunken garden, shall we? Nice and quiet."

Smythe nodded, following them as they led him past the servants' staircase and down the hallway.

HARRY WATCHED AS Smythe tapped out a cigarette and lit it with the hurried movements of a man who had not a second to waste in the task.

He inhaled deeply, then blew out a giant billow of smoke that – in the suddenly still air in the sunken garden – just hung there like an uninvited guest to the serious chat about to commence.

Kat sat down on one of the stone benches in the garden surrounded by a rather comprehensive array of herbs, all used on a regular basis – Harry imagined – by McLeod and his kitchen staff.

Spiky rosemary next to full sprigs of thyme. Great fronds of parsley hanging in a disorganised way near large and stalwart sage plants.

Could make a halfway decent soup just from the ingredients here, Harry thought.

"Mr Smythe," Kat said.

Smythe took another deep drag from his cigarette.

"Do you know of anyone who might want something bad to happen to the *Firefly*, or Amelia?"

Harry could see that Smythe was either totally shocked by the question – or he was doing a damn fine job of pretending he was.

"What? *No.* Of course not! Who would want to harm dear Amelia?" Smythe looked around, shook his head. "That's absolutely ridiculous!"

Ball parried, Harry turned to his wife, legs crossed, the gentlest smile on her face, looking so reassuring, as if Smythe's discounting of that possibility *made perfect sense.*

Nonetheless…

"And yet, Mr Smythe, we have discovered that the *Firefly's* fuel problems yesterday were no accident."

"No?" said Smythe, his eyes showing real alarm, cigarette poised in mid-air.

"No indeed," said Harry, deciding that he wanted to play.

He glanced at Kat for approval of what he was about to say. He saw her nod imperceptibly, and continued.

"Yes. Appears that somebody deliberately tampered with the plane's instruments to show a *false* fuel reading."

"I don't believe it," said Smythe, still not moving.

Kat picked up from Harry. "'Fraid so. Instead of a full tank – Amelia took off with barely enough fuel for twenty minutes' flight."

"Impossible," said Smythe, taking another deep drag on his cigarette.

Harry explained how he and Kat had found the pins in the fuel gauge – and how they then mysteriously disappeared.

All the while, Smythe shaking his head in disbelief.

"Madness," he said. "Sheer madness."

"Indeed, Mr Smythe," said Harry. "So, pardon me for asking you again, but can you think of any reason why someone might want things to go wrong with Amelia's tour?"

For a second, Smythe, his cigarette down to a nub, looked away. Another puff, and he tossed it to the gravel below, about to step on it and grind it into the caramel-coloured stones when he caught Harry's disapproving look

"I say. My aunt's rather partial to this little garden back here. Would you mind awfully disposing of your *butt*, as the Yanks call them – isn't that right, Kat? – in that rather charming metal *cendrier*, over there?"

Harry smiled patiently. Smythe walked dutifully to the cendrier, and tossed what was left of his smoke.

Harry shot Kat a grin.

The way they played this little interrogation game?

So much fun.

When the chastened Smythe returned, Harry continued.

"All right. Now to my question?"

Then it seemed like a light bulb appeared over Smythe's bulbous head, quickly followed by a look of horror, so genuine that it could not be some clever act of dissemblance.

"My gawd! Now that you ask. Yes, there *is*."

Smythe looked from Harry to Kat as if they were dullards, slow to get where this particular flow was leading. Then he looked up at the house, frowned and shook his head.

"But this won't do," he said, turning to peer down at the far end of the sunken garden, where a door was set in the high brick wall. "That door leads out into the grounds, does it?"

"It does," said Harry, surprised. "Are you suggesting this is not private enough?"

"Not for matters as grave as this," said Smythe, his voice dropping dramatically to a near-whisper. "Matters of *national security*."

Harry looked at Kat and shrugged.

"Well then," he said as he stood up and led them both down the garden, through the old door, and out onto the deserted meadows, far behind Mydworth Manor.

9.

HIGH STAKES

AS THEY WALKED away from the manor house, Kat saw, just ahead in the shade of an ancient oak tree, a small round metal table and three chairs.

"I've never been back here, Harry," said Kat as they approached.

"In the summer, when I was a boy," said Harry, as they reached the chairs and dusted them off, "we used to take breakfast right under this tree."

Kat, reached across, touched his hand. "We must do that one morning."

Harry smiled, and then he turned to Smythe, pulled out a chair for him and sat down himself.

"This – private enough?" he said.

"It'll do," said Smythe, lighting another cigarette.

"You were saying?" said Harry.

"Right, yes. Who might have it in for this tour, you ask? Well," he said, looking around and lowering his voice again, "Albion Aero, of course! Isn't it obvious?"

Kat glanced at Harry, then, with her best poker face turned back to Smythe.

"I don't quite understand, Mr Smythe," she said. "Perhaps you could explain?"

"The defence contracts, of course!" said Smythe. "The *Firefly* versus the *Bulldog*!"

"The *Bulldog*?" said Kat, innocently. "I'm still not sure I—"

"Tell you what, chap," said Harry. "Why don't you start at the very beginning – with you how came to be involved with Miss Earhart in the first place?"

"Oh well, that's easy enough to answer. When it comes to organising flying tours, yours truly is, as they say, the *ne plus ultra*."

"You've quite some experience then?" said Kat.

"Experience? Twenty years, my dear. And, before that, some of the nation's most prestigious travelling shows."

Kat caught Harry's eye. Not a flicker. But, like her, he must surely be thinking.

Travelling shows? Does he mean circuses?

"Right then – did Miss Earhart approach you?" said Harry.

"Oh, no," said Smythe. "Sandbourne Aviation came to *me*. Mr Sandbourne himself, no less. He'd heard that Amelia needed a plane – something special – so he made her an offer: free loan of the new *Firefly*, long as he had someone in place – steady and experienced running the show."

"That person being *you*?" said Kat.

"Precisely. He and I go back a long way, you know."

"And what's in it for Sandbourne?" said Harry.

"What *isn't*? They get daily publicity about their wonderful new machine, and – with Amelia in the cockpit – the whole world sees that the *Firefly* can take anything a top pilot can throw at it."

"The whole world," said Harry. "By which you mean the War Office?"

"Exactly," said Smythe. "Next month they're making a decision on which monoplane to purchase."

"Big decision, I imagine?" said Kat.

"Absolutely! Worth millions of pounds," said Smythe.

"And, let me guess," said Harry, "the Albion *Bulldog* is now suddenly not even in the running?"

Smythe laughed, his jowls wobbling as he dabbed his face with his handkerchief.

"Not surprising! Amelia and the *Firefly* – in the news! – have been smiling up at those ministry men from their breakfast tables every day for two weeks."

"Hardly in *The Times*, I imagine," said Harry.

"Who cares about the stuffy old *Times*? Those Whitehall types – you know they read their servants' tabloids, every damn one, cover to cover!"

Kat leaned forward.

"Okay, so what about Albion? What makes you think they might be involved in what happened to Amelia?"

"Look. Stands to reason, doesn't it? They'll not be taking this 'loss' lying down."

"Quite an accusation," said Harry. "I mean – they *are* a blue chip company."

"Blue chip, potato chip," said Smythe. "I'd bet my backside on them being responsible."

Kat watched as Smythe prepared to flick his cigarette butt into the grass – and then clearly thought better of it, snipping the end off with his fingernails like a workman, and dropping it into his jacket pocket.

Beneath this bluster of a tale – could there be any truth in Smythe's accusation? Or more to the point, any evidence?

"But Mr Smythe," she said. "How could they possibly have gotten away with it? I mean – Paddy O'Brien is your man, isn't he? Surely he wouldn't let anyone from Albion near Amelia's plane?"

"Ah yes, Paddy. Hmm. He's a good mechanic, no doubt about that. Damned good, but…"

"Let me guess. For reasons we all know, he has a tendency to take his eye off the ball?" said Harry.

"Sad to say, yes," said Smythe. "When I brought him on board, I wasn't aware how he'd, well, *deteriorated*, since last we worked together."

"You've known him long?" said Harry.

"Since '18. Gave him a job when he came back from the front."

"RAF?" said Harry.

"Apparently. Never talks about it."

Interesting, thought Kat. *O'Brien had been through that hell too. And that – perhaps a reason for the drink problem.*

"Once you realised though, quite a risk?" she said.

"Risk?" said Smythe.

"His problem with drink. Lives in the balance you might say."

"Ahem, indeed. Well. I've had words with him. Read him the Riot Act. Mustn't let the side down, tour of duty nearly over, chin up and so on."

"And you really think that's worked?" said Harry.

"Well, I was sure of it!" said Smythe.

Kat imagined that Smythe's universe didn't allow for much self-doubt. But now he looked much less sure of himself.

"You don't think he might have been responsible for the refuelling error then?" said Kat.

Smythe shook his head. "Even in his cups, O'Brien was always one for keeping a bloody good eye on things, and double-checking. That's for sure. And that includes fixing a damn fuel gauge."

"Okay, but if Albion were behind it, how do you account for the pins disappearing *today*?" said Kat.

"Take a look," said Smythe, gesturing towards the distant meadow where the planes were lined up, spectators and crew dotted around each machine. "See there? Any one of those crewmen could have slipped into the *Firefly* while O'Brien was *distracted*. And most of them have the wherewithal to do it."

Kat looked at Harry, guessing that what Smythe said was true. Almost anybody on the grounds could be a suspect.

Which put them back at square one.

The look on Harry's face showed that he probably agreed. He stood up – meeting over.

"Well, Mr Smythe, I must say, this has been awfully useful," he said. "Can't thank you enough for taking the time to listen to our concerns. Giving us your thoughts."

"Not at all, young man," said Smythe, pulling back his chair and standing too. "Can't have your dear old aunt worrying, now, can we?"

"What if whoever's responsible tries to do it again?" said Kat, getting up.

"Don't you worry about that," said Smythe, his cheery smile fading. "I've told O'Brien not to let that damn plane out of his sight, night and day."

That's reassuring, thought Kat. *Though O'Brien's hardly the best candidate for such a role. And certainly no help if Amelia kept borrowing other planes to try out.*

"You really ought to partake of a little lunch, Mr Smythe, before the staff clear it away," said Harry, tidying the chairs.

"Kind of you."

"Oh – there is one last question," said Harry, smiling at Smythe.

"Fire away."

"I assume you must be responsible for all the day-to-day running costs of the tour?"

"I am indeed," said Smythe, brushing a little ash from his jacket. "And they are no small sums, I can tell you."

"Oh, I'm sure they're not," said Harry. "I imagine you keep tight control though?"

"Every last penny," said Smythe, "because, as we know, look after the pennies…"

"In which case, you'll have a record of the fuel payment you made yesterday to Great Western Aerodrome?"

Kat saw Smythe stop and swivel to face Harry, his brow furrowed. "What?"

"I'm thinking, it must have been a remarkably cheap purchase," said Harry. "Twenty minutes' fuel."

"I don't, er, well, I can't possibly re—"

"Funny you didn't notice," continued Harry, a look of polite enquiry on his face.

Smythe seemed to scramble for the right words.

"Well, I don't always have time to, um, of course—"

"Not to worry if you can't find the paperwork today," said Harry, smiling again. "I've put a call into the aerodrome to check, and they're going to pop a copy of the invoice in the post; should be here in the morning."

"Ah, yes. Good."

Kat looked at Smythe: the man's shoulders had dropped, his whole body deflated like a pricked balloon.

"As I said – do grab some lunch," said Harry, patting Smythe on the shoulder. "Lady Mortimer and I must go see how the rehearsals for the display are coming along."

Then he put an arm around Kat's waist, and together they turned and headed across the meadow towards the stables and the airstrip, leaving Smythe standing alone, motionless.

"WELL, THAT LAST bit? Neatly done," said Kat, as soon as they were out of earshot. "Clever trick."

"Wasn't it?" said Harry. "Saw it in one of those gangster flicks. Detective heads to the door, turns and lobs a question into the room like a grenade, waits for reaction. Boom!"

"Certainly worked on Smythe!"

"Ha, I know. That face?"

"Hand in the cookie jar if ever I saw one," said Kat. "By the way, did you really order a copy of the invoice?"

"I did," said Harry. "But it'll take a week at least for them to dig it out and get it to me."

"He's not to know that?"

"Exactly," said Harry, laughing. "Chap's guilty as hell all right. Though I'm not quite sure exactly *what* he's guilty of."

"But, Harry – why the stuff about Albion? Was that just to cover his own tracks?"

"I have absolutely no idea," said Harry. "But I'll tell you one thing. Something's definitely going on, and I don't think Amelia or the *Firefly* are safe."

"I agree. And right now, I don't think she should trust anybody. Not even the people closest to her."

"Not sure she has much choice though – she can't do without O'Brien for instance."

"Does Smythe's story match his?"

"Pretty much," said Harry. "Chap told me he'd been through a rough patch in the last couple of years – and Smythe gave him a second chance."

"Think that's true?" said Kat. "Smythe's not somebody I'd credit with offering second chances."

"Me neither."

Together they approached the improvised landing ground, where Kat saw a small crowd strung out along the tiny airstrip.

"What's going on?" she said, as they both quickened their step.

"I have no idea. Whatever it is, it's got everybody watching."

In the distance was the throaty sound of a plane's engine revving.

"I say," said Harry, shading his eyes from the afternoon sun. "Look."

Kat peered in the direction of the sound. At the far end of the grass runway, a couple of hundred yards away, she spotted a small plane taxiing and turning, ready to take off.

"Well – I do believe that's Amelia," said Harry.

"I thought the *Firefly* was grounded?"

"It is. But that's not the *Firefly*. That's the new de Havilland she was talking about."

Kat heard a gutsy growl from the plane's engine, and saw it lurch forward at the far end of the runway, like a horse bolting under starter's orders.

The shape, smooth and streamlined, just like the *Firefly*: one single wing supported on struts, behind a massive engine and propeller.

"Watch carefully," said Harry. "I suspect our new friend is about to show us what she's made of."

10.

AN UNEXPECTED DISPLAY

AS KAT WATCHED Amelia in the de Havilland, racing towards them from the far end of the field, Harry took her hand.

In acknowledgement, she gave it a squeeze.

"Exciting, no? Seeing this amazing woman taking to the air?" said Harry.

Kat nodded and had a fleeting thought: *Harry is quite taken with his fellow pilot.*

But she quickly pushed that pesky idea well away.

With an incredible roar from the engine, the de Havilland seemed to simply *pop* into the air, just a few feet away from them both. Amelia got the nose of the plane up, and suddenly she was making a direct line towards a distant bank of puffy white clouds.

But such a straight line didn't last long. Kat saw Amelia first make the wings wobble back and forth, approximating a wave.

Then she had the plane do a slow, lazy bank to the left, before sending it flying right over them.

As one, the crowd lining the airstrip spun round, to see the de Havilland pass barely twenty feet above Mydworth Manor, before climbing steeply into the blue, cloud-dotted sky.

Kat watched Harry.

This flying – something he misses, she guessed.

Maybe we need do something about that?

And without removing his eyes from the plane as it soared far overhead, Harry said: "I will tell you one thing – that woman can fly anything."

And while Kat didn't understand what was actually involved in piloting an aircraft, she had to admit it was kind of wonderful to see the plane circling high above as if it were a great raptor, commanding it all.

She looked along the line at the crowd of pilots, crew and early guests who were also watching this prelude to what – tomorrow – would be a full-on aerial display.

"Come on, Harry," she said. "Let's go do some detective work."

And together they walked the length of the grass runway to the stables, where the other planes were parked.

AS THEY APPROACHED the *Firefly*, Kat saw Pidge watching the display – for once standing alone. Twenty yards away, Greene and Smythe sat hunched together at a table, deep in conversation, papers spread out between them.

"No sign of O'Brien," said Harry.

Kat looked around. "So much for security. Maybe in the stables working on a part?"

"Or in his quarters working on a bottle."

Kat shook her head. "Let's hope not." Then, with a nod to Harry, she walked to Pidge, who stood – neck craned – peering up into the sky.

"Hello Miss Earhart," said Kat as she and Harry drew up next to her.

"Oh – Lady Mortimer," said Pidge, turning quickly. "Sir Harry."

"Please," said Harry, smiling. "Kat and Harry – no need to stand on ceremony."

"Oh well, yes. If you're sure," said the young woman. "And do call me 'Pidge' – I always look round for Amelia when people say 'Miss Earhart'!"

"Pidge it is, then," said Kat. Then she looked up to where Amelia was performing a series of slow, rolling loops across the sky. "Your sister – she's quite something, isn't she?"

"Oh, don't I know it. Unstoppable. Can't keep her out of the air."

"You ever get nervous watching her?"

"Never. She *knows* what she's doing. Always has."

Kat motioned towards Greene and Smythe. "And Mr Greene – not taking pictures today?"

"He said he doesn't need any pictures of the de Havilland. Only the *Firefly*."

Kat nodded, guessing it must be part of the reporter's contract.

"You must have seen your sister do plenty of displays," said Harry. "This – right now – the standard routine?"

"Pretty much," said Pidge. "Oh, do watch – this bit's always fun!"

Kat shaded her eyes – to see the plane reaching the top of its loop, then slowing, slowing, engine silent, until it seemed to be clawing at the air, before falling in a clumsy, tumbling mock-stall towards the ground.

"Ahem! Makes me feel queasy just watching," said Kat as, just before it seemed it must hit the ground, the engine kicked in, the plane levelled and then shot back into the sky. For a few seconds it disappeared completely into the sun.

"You must have been worried yesterday, when Amelia had to crash land?" said Harry.

"A little, yes," said Pidge, turning to look at them both, her face now serious.

"Did she say anything at all about what might have gone wrong?" said Kat.

"Not really. Only, she said it was her own fault," said Pidge with a shrug. "Said O'Brien warned her there was some kind of problem with the gauge but she ignored him."

Kat caught Harry's eye. The mechanic might be a drunk, but it seemed he had at least done part of his duty.

"But you didn't notice anything funny yesterday at the aerodrome?"

"*Funny?*"

"Unusual, perhaps," said Harry.

Pidge seemed to consider this for a few moments, then: "No," she said. "Though I didn't get there until the last minute. Had to get a cab from the hotel."

"Why was that?" said Kat.

Pidge shrugged. "Ronnie and Mr Smythe had some boring meeting to go to first."

"Boring meetings?" came Greene's voice – and Kat turned to see the journalist suddenly standing now right behind them. "I'm sure no meeting with me in it can ever be boring!"

"Ha, never, Ronnie, never!" said Pidge, grinning at him. "But you know what I mean."

"I'm sure I do," said Greene putting his hand on her shoulder.

The sudden throaty sound of the de Havilland's engine stopped all conversation, and they watched as the plane appeared from behind a fold in the hills and came racing towards them, parallel to the crowd, at tree-top height.

Suddenly the wing tip flipped ninety degrees – and the plane was flying sideways. Then it flipped again – so the de Havilland passed them flat-out and upside down.

"Absolutely amazing," said Harry, as the plane roared back up into the sky.

"Better believe it," said Greene. "And tomorrow? In the *Firefly*? Can only be better."

"That's funny," said Pidge, still watching the de Havilland climbing higher and higher. "That upside down bit? That's usually her finale."

"Hey – you're right," said Greene. "What's she up to?"

Kat looked at Harry – he shook his head, as if he too had no idea. She turned back to look up into the sky, where Amelia was still climbing at speed.

"What's this?" came another voice next to them, and Kat saw Smythe at her side, also peering up into the sky.

"Little addition to the routine, I believe," said Greene.

"Well – she hasn't talked to me about it," said Smythe, not hiding his irritation.

Kat heard the engine tone change – and she looked up: the de Havilland barely a dot against the blue.

"Oh," said Harry. "I do believe she's going to dive."

And now, as the distant engine noise increased, Kat could see that little dot pinned against the sky, as the plane seemed to reach the very top of its arc…

… hang in the air for a second…

and then flip over, point towards the ground and accelerate.

Faster and faster, tearing towards the solid earth, the engine noise now furious, urgent, insistent, as if daring the earth below to rise to meet it.

"Good *Lord*," said Harry, and Kat stepped closer to him, put her arm through his.

"What the hell speed is she doing?" said Greene.

"My guess?" said Harry. "Three-fifty. Four hundred?"

Kat tried to imagine Amelia in that tiny, juddering cockpit – and her view of the Sussex countryside *racing* towards her.

"Gosh," said Pidge.

Kat glanced left and right – the whole crowd now silent, all eyes on the de Havilland racing earthwards like a bullet.

"Think though, um, she really ought to be thinking about pulling out soon," said Harry.

What if she doesn't? thought Kat, gripping Harry tighter.

And even Harry, with all his experience, was alarmed at this.

"Stress on those wings must be extraordinary," he said.

"What do you mean?" said Kat.

She saw Harry glance quickly at Pidge, then lower his voice.

"When she pulls up? De Havilland not made of the right stuff? The speed could tear the wings right off."

Kat's eyes locked on the plane as it now seemed impossibly close, as if just seconds away from disaster.

"Now, Amelia," said Harry, quietly, almost as if to himself. "Come on. *Now.*"

And on cue, Kat saw the nose of the plane pull up, the engine racing, and with a great whoosh, the de Havilland arced up and out of its dive just a hundred feet above their heads, and looped back into the sky.

And the whole crowd as one roared and cheered and waved.

"Well, well – how about that?" said Harry. "Talk about a finale!"

Kat swallowed hard, and realised she'd been holding her breath all this time. She looked over at Pidge who was laughing and joking with Greene. The young woman caught Kat's eye.

"See, Lady Mortimer, er, Kat?" said Pidge. "Nothing to worry about!"

"If you say so," said Kat, laughing. "I don't think I could bear to watch that again!"

"Think we might well have to tomorrow," said Harry.

"You think so?" said Greene, turning his attention away from Amelia's sister.

"Now she's tried it out on the de Havilland, I'd bet she'll want to see how the *Firefly* handles the manoeuvre," said Harry.

"Damn risky," said Smythe, joining them. "Something new like that. But I must admit – a cracking way to end the show."

Cracking? thought Kat. *Yes, as long as nothing goes wrong.*

11.

A DELICATE SITUATION

DISPLAY OVER, KAT watched Amelia head due south before making a much sharper turn, to line the plane up for its landing on Aunt Lavinia's well-manicured field.

All eyes were still on the plane, as it gently lowered. And when the wheels hit the tightly cut grass of the field, that landing was so soft the plane barely kicked up any dust into the air.

In moments, Amelia had the plane taxiing towards the stables near all the other new arrivals: some vintage, some more recent, all lined up.

"And after all that – that landing?" said Harry, turning to Kat and smiling. "Wow."

Despite the glow in Harry's eyes, Kat felt not a drop of jealousy. *Wow indeed.*

She watched Pidge, Greene and Smythe rush over to where the plane had stopped, as Amelia popped out of the cockpit, grinning. Other pilots clustered nearby, offering comments and congratulations.

Kat wished she had a camera to take a picture of it all. "So, what now, Harry? Head over there? Give Amelia our congrats as well?"

Harry turned to her. "I think she'll be busy talking through the routine with the other pilots, commenting on the plane."

"Guess this isn't a good time to tell her what we've found?"

Harry's eyes narrowed.

"Now? No. I think perhaps this evening at the cocktail reception we can find a moment. A quick – and private – word of caution."

"In the meantime, maybe plan how we can protect her and the *Firefly*."

"Exactly."

Kat took Harry's arm and they left the crowd, walking past the stables back towards the house and the cars.

As they did, another plane flew low over the house, its engine just meekly ticking over – in stark contrast to the roar of the de Havilland during the display.

But like the de Havilland, Kat could see those same lines, so clean, so beautiful, so *modern*.

Harry paused to look up, and Kat saw him shield his eyes against the sun as he watched the plane arc away then turn to make a landing on the field.

"Well, well," he said. "I wondered when she'd turn up."

"What is it?"

"That aircraft? The *Bulldog*," said Harry. "Albion aiming to grab some publicity on the back of Amelia's tour."

"Smythe won't be happy," said Kat.

"Oh, I don't know. As long as the *Firefly* looks the better plane, Amelia on the stick, thrilling us all – his job's *done*."

"Yes, but doesn't that mean more pressure on Amelia to push it to its limits?" said Kat, suddenly feeling a pang of anxiety.

"True. But after what we just witnessed? I'd trust her to know those limits."

Kat hesitated a moment before adding one unsettling thought.

"As long as nobody messes with her plane."

"Ah yes," said Harry.

They set off again towards the house.

"So," Kat repeated, suddenly aware, as the expression went, that something else was afoot here, "what now?"

"Well, we do need to change for this cocktail party."

"Shouldn't take long," Kat suggested. "Although there's the added time of driving to the Dower House and back again."

"True enough. But I had a feeling things might get a little rushed this afternoon, so I took the liberty of asking Maggie to drop our evening clothes here at the house."

"Oh, did you now?" said Kat.

"Thought you wouldn't mind," said Harry. "Our usual room in the manor house is all made up too."

"That a fact?"

"You see, I thought we might need a little extra time to… freshen up, yes?"

And at that, he took her hand, and Kat rewarded both his plans and that grasp with a broad smile.

"Freshen up? Is *that* what it's called?"

And Harry, now leading her towards the house laughed. "Works for me. You too?"

And in answer, all Kat did was give his hand a firm squeeze, afternoon plans *quite in place*.

But then – as if popping that wonderful bubble – Benton appeared on the main steps.

"Awfully sorry, sir," he said. "But we appear to have a little *problem* with one of the guests."

"Can it wait?" said Harry

"I'm afraid not, sir."

"All right, Benton, be with you in a second," said Harry, and Kat saw the butler turn and head back towards the house.

Kat looked at Harry. He returned the look – and raised his eyebrows. She smiled.

"Guess the 'freshening up' will have to wait?" she said.

"It'll be all the better for that, I'm sure," he said, and they both turned and followed Benton.

INSIDE THE HOUSE, Kat could see that preparations for the evening's cocktail party and dinner were already well under way.

Down the long corridor that led to the ballroom, servants passed one another in a constant stream, carrying trays of plates, glasses, linen.

All dutifully halted to let them pass, as she and Harry followed Benton down the back stairs to the lower ground floor.

Benton striding purposefully, silent.

Past the servants' hall and the kitchens, a bustle of noise, chatter, and a myriad of wonderful smells of cooking, until they reached the butler's pantry – Benton's domain.

Benton opened the door – but not fully – just enough for Kat and Harry to slip in after him.

Kat wondered why the need for discretion, but as the door closed behind her and she took in the room, with its cupboards, shelves, locked store and large safe, she saw the other two occupants.

McLeod the cook, standing, arms folded, face grim. And slumped at a small table in the middle of the room – O'Brien, Amelia's mechanic.

The table, bare but for a single bottle of whisky – nearly empty.

"McLeod," said Harry, nodding to the man.

"Sir Harry," said McLeod.

"And Mr O'Brien," said Harry. "This is quite a surprise."

Kat saw O'Brien glance up at Harry then look away shamefaced.

"Care to tell me what this is about?" said Harry, turning to Benton.

"I think Mr McLeod is better placed to enlighten you, sir," said Benton.

"As you wish," said McLeod, his Scottish burr sometimes teetering on the incomprehensible to Kat. "And I'm not happy getting any man into trouble, sir, but this is something neither I nor Mr Benton felt we could keep *below stairs*."

"I understand," said Harry. "Carry on."

"As you might imagine sir, what with the party and the dinner, things have been a trifle hectic down here this afternoon. Half an hour ago, I was passing Mr Benton's pantry, when I heard a noise from within."

McLeod paused. Kat guessed he was a man who could keep a secret, especially if it related to the staff.

But this...

"That room is of course, always locked when Mr Benton is above stairs, what with the safe and so on, and nobody has authority to enter without Mr Benton overseeing. But, as I said, hearing that noise, and upon opening the door and entering the pantry, I espied Mr O'Brien here standing, drinking from *that bottle*."

"I see," said Harry. "And the bottle, Benton?"

"From my cupboard here, sir. No doubt about that." Benton sniffed. "I very carefully monitor the inventory."

"Right then," said Harry.

Kat could see him weighing up the situation. O'Brien certainly not a servant. But nor was he an official guest who would be joining the others at the party.

Bit of a grey area there.

"Mr McLeod, Benton – thank you. You did the right thing calling me down here. Does anyone else know about this?"

"No sir," said Benton.

"Think it's best for all if we keep a lid on it, yes? I'll take it from here."

Then he turned to O'Brien.

"A word outside, Mr O'Brien if you please."

And O'Brien, still silent, stood up and followed as Harry led the way out of the kitchens, up the stairs, through the hall, and out onto the gravel drive in front of the house.

Outside, the afternoon sun was still warm.

Overhead Kat caught sight of a pair of biplanes, making lazy patterns in the sky. In the bright light, she could see O'Brien's eyes bloodshot, and a sheen of sweat on his brow.

"All right then, O'Brien. This is a bit of a mess you and your drinking has stirred up here, isn't it?" said Harry.

"Yes, sir."

"Stealing liquor from the house – apart from the damage you do to Miss Earhart, I mean – I should really have you up before the courts, man."

"Yes, sir. Sorry, sir."

"If you needed booze so badly, couldn't you have just sent one of the lads into the village to simply buy you a bottle?"

O'Brien didn't reply – and Kat guessed he hadn't wanted to reveal his addiction. She caught Harry's eye, hoping he would recognise in her face a plea for clemency.

"Right then," Harry said, with a look to Kat. "I'll do you a deal."

"Sir?"

"If you stay off the bottle until this show's over, and if you keep a damn tight eye on Amelia and her plane, then we'll forget this whole damn thing happened."

"Sir?" said O'Brien, his eyes suddenly wider, and Kat sensed a weight lifted from his shoulders.

Then – an odd frown on the reprieved man's face. "But – what do you mean? Keep an eye on the   plane? Is there a problem?"

"No. Not that we know of. But let's just say, there's a nasty rumour going round that someone might have it in for the *Firefly*," said Kat.

"What?"

"We don't know much more than that," said Kat. "A bit of fear. Some suspicion. But I hope we can rely on your help?"

"You can, Lady Mortimer. Sir Harry."

"Right then. Good man," said Harry. "Now, you'd better get over there, get to work."

Kat watched O'Brien turn on his heels and scurry off towards the stables and the line of planes. Then she turned back to Harry.

"You think we can trust him to stay on the wagon?" she said.

"Doubtful," said Harry. "But he's scared. And I think even if he's fast asleep under the plane he might just deter someone up to no good."

She saw him check his watch.

"Well, well. Just time to freshen up, I think," she said.

"Oh yes," said Harry, smiling. "*Plenty*."

And they walked hand in hand back to the house, as overhead another biplane puttered across the sky.

12.

NIGHT FALLS IN MYDWORTH

HARRY PAUSED AT the bedroom door and turned to Kat before he opened it.

"So – how do I look?"

Kat grinned. "Aren't *I* supposed to ask *you* that question?"

"Well, yes. But let's face it. You *always* look smashing. Me? Starched shirt, black tie, shoes polished to within an inch of their lives – always feels more like a uniform!"

He opened the door, and mock bowed to Kat as she passed through onto the wide landing of Mydworth Manor.

Then she took his arm, as together they walked down the graceful curved staircase, past those now-familiar portraits of Harry's ancestors, the bubbly sounds of the cocktail party below drifting up towards them.

"You? In evening dress, Harry? Comes off just fine."

"That's a relief. Must uphold the Mortimer standard for sartorial excellence."

"And me? Your answer, please?"

And before they reached the bottom of the stairs, Harry paused and turned to her. He leaned forward.

"*Fantastic*. If I wasn't already married to you, I'd get down on one knee right now."

Kat laughed.

"Not on the stairs, of course," he said, taking her arm again and leading her down. "Not a complete fool for love!"

She loved that he had that effect, mixing shameless flirting with humour. *They don't make men like Harry back in the Bronx,* she thought.

They passed a ramrod-straight footman who stood as if guarding the hallway.

"Lady Mortimer, Sir Harry." He bowed his head.

And in they went.

HARRY LOOKED AROUND the crowded saloon, filled with impeccably dressed guests, some with champagne flutes in hand, others nursing small martini glasses. A cellist and violinist played somewhere near the back of the room.

Benton stood to one side, near the entrance to the dining room, surveying it all.

Kat leaned in to Harry. "There's our Mr Greene. Looks as smooth and slick as ever in evening dress."

"With Pidge, I see. Certainly, doing nothing to hide his interest."

"Oh," Kat said, "don't look now, but Smythe is about to make some kind of cheesy thing vanish."

"One must feed the fires of promotion."

"You know who these people are?"

"Some. At least by face if not name. Plenty of them with real money, that's for sure. Ideally all set to make Smythe's attaché case even fatter."

A young man – who actually looked more like a boy – came over directly with a tray of flutes, the bubbles all streaming up as if in a mad race to the surface.

"Champagne, m'lady, Sir Harry?"

"Excellent idea," Harry said taking two flutes, and handing one to Kat.

That first sip.

"Oh," Kat said. "This is good."

"Yes, my aunt learned a few things in her years in Paris. She gives old Benton quite *specific* instructions on what champagne to offer at her parties."

"We must get some of this as well."

Harry turned to her. "Consider it done."

But he saw that Kat was still looking around, the chatter and music mixing, all very festive. Lavinia over to the side surrounded by a trio of couples, all dressed to perfection.

"Harry – I don't see Amelia anywhere. This is kind of her party, no?"

"Wonder where she is."

"We do need to have that little chat with her."

"Right. Let me go and ask Lavinia if she's down yet."

Harry walked over to his aunt and her cluster of well-heeled guests.

KAT WATCHED LAVINIA deftly give her nearby guests a smile as Harry stood close, probably asking if he could have a word.

Then she walked away, following Harry to a quiet corner of the room, and Kat joined them.

Lavinia looked right at Kat.

"What is it? Something wrong?"

Kat gave her a smile. She and Harry had alerted Lavinia to their concerns during the morning, but also decided not to worry her overly.

"No. All good. I mean, we are digging into things, with Amelia's plane, but—"

Harry quickly added. "As of now, nothing substantial yet."

She saw Lavinia fix Harry with her eyes, a look that said that she didn't miss a trick.

"The use of the word 'yet' is *not* the most promising one to hear in this situation."

Harry continued: "We wondered if you'd seen Amelia? Wanted a word. Nothing urgent, but—"

Lavinia nodded.

"Harry, Kat… look around. Quite a crowd…"

"Lovely party as usual, Aunt Lavinia," said Kat. "Quite looking forward to whatever McLeod has planned."

"I believe lamb. Not my favourite. Though McLeod loves cooking nothing more."

And then Kat realised where Lavinia was going with this.

"Ah - this party… Guessing a little tricky for Amelia?"

"I'll *say*. That young woman may fly the globe. Get photographed, interviewed, all that. But an event like this? Even with the goal of raising money for her organisation?"

"Deer in the headlights?" Kat said.

Lavinia smiled at that. "We say rabbit, but yes. That is exactly what I meant. All dressed up – she's beautiful of course. But out of her flying garb – decidedly uncomfortable."

"So – she's still in her room?" Harry said

At that, Lavinia laughed and rolled her eyes.

"No. I told her I could have Huntley drive her into Mydworth. Explore the town, as long as she got back before dinner. She absolutely *must* say a few words to get everyone all set for tomorrow and opening their wallets."

Kat saw Harry tilt his head. "She's in Mydworth?"

"Yes, and I imagine decidedly happier. I'm sure you can wait till she returns."

"I think we'll pop down there," said Harry, turning to her. "Huntley in the Bentley? Shouldn't be too hard to find."

"Oh dear – that all sounds rather urgent!" said Lavinia, her face falling. "You *have* learned something, haven't you? Something worrisome?"

Harry put a hand on Lavinia's arm. "Just as soon as Kat and I really know anything, we'll tell you."

"Please do. Always preferable to have the host informed if anything untoward has happened."

Kat resisted the temptation to add *may happen*.

"Don't worry, we'll find her. Make sure she's back here for dinner as you planned."

Lavinia smiled.

"And meanwhile," she said, "I shall go back to keeping the champagne and caviar coming. As they say, the show – even without its star – must go on."

And she turned back to her guests.

Kat took a breath and said: "Let's go find Amelia."

IT DIDN'T TAKE long to locate the black Bentley – parked right on the High Street, quite near the town hall.

Huntley stood leaning against the shiny black hood of the car, smoking a cigarette.

But with no Amelia in sight.

Kat pulled the Alvis into a space just behind the Bentley.

Harry was quickly out of the car, Kat behind him.

"I say, Huntley, my aunt said you were showing Amelia the sights of Mydworth?"

Huntley looked startled to see them.

"Um, Sir Harry, m'lady, yes. I think that big party, all those people, a bit much—"

"Yes, yes," said Harry. "But do you know where she is right *now*?"

"Why yes. She's—"

And Kat saw the man turn, and point at the building just a bit rather down the road. The sign all lit up.

The Electric Pavilion Cinema.

"The talkies? She's in there?"

"Yes. I mean, she saw what was playing" – Huntley pointed to the name on the marquee: *The Thirteenth Chair,* starring Conrad Nagel – "and said she simply *must* see it!"

Kat saw Harry look at her. "Okay, Huntley, we can take it from here. You head back and ask Benton to tell my aunt we'll make sure Amelia returns in time for dinner and fundraising."

"Yes, sir."

And at that, Huntley got into the Bentley, and Harry turned to Kat.

"Fancy taking in a picture show?"

She smiled.

"Of course."

And together they entered the cinema, went to the box office, and bought a pair of tickets from a skinny man in a checked bow tie on what looked to be a slow night at the local movie palace.

ONCE INSIDE, KAT could see the theatre, not very full, the picture flickering, but the projected scene set outside, on a dark night.

So no way to spot Amelia, the fog of cigarette smoke making the task even more difficult.

Harry came close, whispered. "Can't see her. Don't want to just go up and down the rows searching."

"That would hardly do. Just wait a bit. Bound to get brighter."

And for few moments, they stood there, the characters on screen discussing a séance, of all things, to trap a murderer.

Interesting.

But then, the scene changed, to an interior with bright lights.

"Ah—" Harry said. "*There* she is. And what luck, seats on either side."

Kat started walking down the side aisle, past patrons, their eyes glued to the screen. Reaching Amelia's row, she gingerly stepped past a patron who held a half-eaten bar of something in his hand.

He grumbled disapproval at the manoeuvre. Harry meanwhile came in from the far end of the aisle so they could both have a word with the runaway aviatrix.

Kat sat down, and it was only a second before Amelia turned to her. "Kat? What—"

She turned to see Harry on the other side.

"Oops. I'm not in any trouble, am I?"

And Amelia's grin was wide in the reflected light of the screen.

"Not at all," said Kat. "Just Harry and I wanted a word with you. Before you head back."

Amelia's face fell. "Can it wait until the movie is over? It's a mystery, you see, and I absolutely *love* mysteries."

Well, Kat thought, *we have a doozy for you.*

She leaned forward so she could catch Harry, looking on, not really able to make out what was being negotiated.

"Sure. We'll wait. Can't be too much long—" Kat started, but a woman from a few rows back responded with a loud *shoosh*, like a steam valve being realised.

She gave the woman a smile, then turned back.

She then tried to make sense of the movie's plot, having joined it midway, and had very little luck there.

WHEN THE CREDITS began to roll, she took Amelia's hand.

"Come on. You'll be recognised if we wait. Best we go now."

She saw Harry had been thinking he same thing, quickly standing up, moving to the aisle.

She led Amelia out, the stale air of the theatre quickly replaced by a cool summer night.

Like leaving one world for another, Kat thought.

Once outside, Amelia looked around. "Where's that nice Huntley? Said he'd wait."

"Told him we'd get you back," said Harry. "Which we will, of course. But we have to have rather a difficult conversation with you first."

They walked along the street, Kat aware that in evening dress, they probably looked like they had stepped off the movie screen themselves.

A man across the street was sweeping the sidewalk outside of what looked like a small grocery store. He paused to look at them – what had to be, in his mind, one very curious sight.

As they neared the Alvis, Kat said, "Harry, can you tell Amelia what we found? About the *Firefly*?" She hesitated. "And what it may mean."

Harry took a breath.

Not easy to tell a pilot that someone, somehow, tried to make your plane crash.

And that they might well try again.

13.

A REAL MYDWORTH MYSTERY

HARRY PULLED THE Alvis in front of the manor house. He turned back to look at Amelia in the back seat, looking uncomfortable in the role of passenger.

"Running a bit late, so you'd best hurry in."

She nodded. He and Kat had explained to Amelia everything that they had learned, and yet – with all the wide-eyed innocence she could muster – Amelia had simply said, "I can't see anyone wanting to harm me or my plane. It just doesn't make any *sense*."

As she popped out, like a reverse Cinderella hurrying to the festive ballroom dinner inside, Harry turned to Kat.

"What do you think?"

"Wish I had her confidence that all is 'okay'."

"We'd better get in there as well," said Harry, opening his door. "Don't want to miss the star of evening as she makes her pitch to Lavinia's array of fat cats."

He got out, followed by Kat who took his arm as they raced inside to the elaborate buffet dinner, all waiting for the amazing Amelia Earhart to speak.

HARRY LOOKED AT Amelia on the raised dais that Lavinia had arranged. The room was positively bursting with guests, all of whom shared one thing in common.

Money.

As for Amelia, though her voice was thin, almost timid, even faltering here and there, Harry could detect no signs of any nervousness or worry. *So much for their alarms.*

Dinner over, people were now moving around, clustering to hear the speech. He slipped around the high table, and sat next to Kat.

"How was dinner?"

"Great fun. And that dish, the dessert – you call it a *trifle?* – McLeod should get a medal. These weekend 'do's' of your aunt, always good for gaining a few pounds at least."

Harry laughed, then brought his attention back to Amelia.

She was delivering what sounded like a carefully rehearsed text.

"As all of you know, what the Ninety-Nines will do is not only show the world that a woman can *fly*" – Harry saw a small smile on her face; this pause obviously rehearsed – "but that women can do anything. And will!"

The room burst into applause.

"They love her," said Kat.

He turned to his wife, a bit of a glow still on her cheeks.

"What's not to love?" said Harry quickly scanning the room. "I imagine they will be dumping boatloads of cash onto Amelia and her 'Ninety-Nines'." Then he took a breath. "Us too, eh?"

"*Absolutely.*"

Harry scanned the room properly now, took in the well-heeled crowd fully for the first time.

And saw someone he knew.

AMELIA WAS WRAPPING UP.

"Tomorrow I hope you'll join me as I round off Lady Lavinia's charity air festival, with my own display in the wonderful airplane, 'The *Firefly*'. I don't think you'll be disappointed."

More cheering. Harry glanced across the room again at the table that had interested him.

"Harry – what is it?" said Kat, next to him.

He turned to her, a tilt of the head.

"Seen someone I know, actually. Table over there. Fellow with dark hair."

"Dashing-looking chap on the end?" said Kat.

"That's the one."

"Let me guess," said Kat, smiling. "Pilots?"

"So it would seem."

"Know him from…?"

Harry turned back to her. "RAF. Terry Crichton. One of the best pilots I ever encountered. I'm thinking a little chat might be useful."

"Shall I come too?"

But Harry turned to the dais, where Lavinia was holding Amelia's hands in hers, tightly, as others gathered near for a word with the famous aviatrix.

Smythe to one side, discreetly relieving the guests of envelopes of cash.

"This'll be breaking up soon. Think we'd best keep a watch on things outside, don't you?"

"*Gotcha*. I'll slip away. Meet you down by the stables when you've had your chat?"

"Great." Harry stood up. "I say, you find him 'dashing'?"

"Oh yes. Even from across the room."

"Really?"

"Pilot too. Hmm."

And Kat laughed as she too got up, and grinning, walked away from their table, everyone else's eyes on Amelia.

"TERRY?" HARRY SAID, approaching the table.

He saw his fellow pilot look up.

"Thought you had to be banging around here somewhere, Harry."

"Yes, my aunt does like me to make the occasional appearance now and then."

Harry scanned the other young men at Crichton's table, looking up. Either curious or perhaps impressed by 'Sir Harry's' appearance.

"Terry – got a few minutes, old chap? Something I could use your thoughts on."

"Absolutely." He stood up. "Been dying for a cigarette, anyway. Was informed that the ballroom was strictly no-smoking."

Harry grinned. "Yes. My aunt has some rather modern ideas about the healthfulness of smoking. Though I do believe port and cigars *are* scheduled for later."

Terry came beside him, and Harry saw the tell-tale limp, remembering how, after being shot down, Crichton returned to the squadron, not about to let a mere leg wound keep him out of the air.

Harry matched his pace as he led him to the back of the ballroom, past hallways and corridors, to a door that led out.

Where they could speak unnoticed, and unheard.

KAT WAITED A politic few moments, then stood up to head out to where the planes and pilots were clustered, leaving the glittering party behind.

As she moved to the side of the ballroom, she saw Lavinia catch her eye.

Her look implied she was perhaps curious as to what Kat was doing, and maybe also noting that her nephew had also disappeared.

Kat forced a reassuring smile, though she knew that she wasn't at *all* reassured herself.

As she passed the chattering crowd, she noticed that someone *wasn't* there.

Ronald Greene.

Could be a lot of explanations for where he might be, she thought.

And then, achieving as much speed as she could in her tight evening gown – all a shimmering turquoise, with heels that were certainly unused to navigating at such a pace – Kat made her way out to the night.

To where the *Firefly* would be waiting.

Hopefully under the guardianship of O'Brien.

"SO, HARRY," SAID Crichton, lighting a cigarette, flicking the petrol lighter shut. "Domestic life looks like it agrees with you. Must say, your wife? Couldn't help but notice. Well done, I'll say."

Harry grinned at that.

"Domestic life – all good, Terry. You tied the knot yet?"

"Oh, been close a couple of times," said Crichton, blowing a puff of smoke into the chill night. "Can't stay out of the cockpit, though. Which seems to put off any potential brides-to-be for some reason."

"Not surprised, the way *you* fly" said Harry, laughing.

"Oh – I learned from the master," said Terry, slapping Harry on the shoulder. "So, what can I do for you?"

"Bit of a delicate situation; could do with your take."

"Fire away."

"You been mixing with the crews out there?"

"Hard not to, old chap," said Terry. "Pretty much everyone wants a squint at the *Bulldog*."

Harry stopped dead. *So it* was *Crichton who'd been piloting the Albion plane earlier.*

"What's up?" said Terry, clearly seeing Harry's reaction.

96

"Didn't know you were working for Albion these days?"

"What? Me a company man?" said Terry, smiling. "Hell no. I just turn up when they want to show off the *Bulldog*. Fling it round the sky a bit, take the money and run."

"For which, I imagine they pay you handsomely?"

"You bet. Been a bit of a lifesaver. Every couple of weeks I get the call, pop over to Albion, take the kite off to some display or other."

"And the pay cheque?

"Well, let's say suitably *large*."

Harry kept his smile on. His next question, an indelicate one.

"Been doing it a while?"

"On, off, few months. Why?"

"I'm just wondering about this competition between the two planes, the *Bulldog*, the *Firefly*."

"Competition? Think with Amelia's amazing displays these last couple of weeks, *that's* just about over."

"Lot at stake?"

Crichton took another deep drag of his cigarette; more of an effort to buy some time to select the proper response.

"*Boatloads* of cash, old man. Multi-year contract with the government. The highest of stakes."

Harry nodded. "Which is why I wanted to ask you, do you think anyone at Albion would go so far as to… make something bad to happen to Amelia's plane?"

That – Harry saw – gave the pilot pause.

"What makes you say that? If you don't mind me asking."

Fair enough, Harry thought.

And he told Terry about the sabotaged fuel gauge and Amelia's crash-landing.

14.

SECRETS IN THE NIGHT

KAT STEPPED OFF the brick steps onto a path that would wind its way down to the stables where most of the pilots gathered – least the ones not flying for one of the big aviation companies.

The glow of fires could be seen, and also the pale light from the windows of the stables which also held the temporary quarters for some of the flyers.

She found that her heels had a knack for finding little ruts and dips in the path, to the point where she finally stopped, slipped them off and – as painful as it might be – made her way in stockinged feet down to the planes.

Said stockings likely to be tattered and useless after the evening's recce.

Not for the first time, she thought.

She could see the *Firefly*, parked some distance from the other planes, catching some of the flickering lights from the camp fires.

Hidden in the shadows, careful not to catch any of that light – she crept closer, looking for O'Brien. But she didn't see anyone standing guard near the plane, watching over it.

Then with one more step onto some loose pebbles that almost made her yelp, she did at last spot the plane's engineer.

Curled up on the ground, snoring loudly.

Sleeping off another night's drinking? she thought. *Even after what they'd said to him?*

She was about to go to him, remind him of his charge to keep his eyes open, when she spotted something odd, to the right, that suddenly caught her eye.

A figure not far from the *Firefly*, crouched in the shadows, hidden. *Another pilot?* she thought. *But why hide in the dark?*

For a second she regretted coming up here alone. There'd already been one act of cold-blooded sabotage on the plane.

If the person responsible was now out there in the darkness, they might have no qualms about using violence – on her too.

But Kat knew there wasn't a way to get help without alerting them. All she could do was hope that the same steely darkness would hide her.

Heart thumping, crouched low, Kat started edging towards the mysterious figure, whoever they might be.

HARRY LOOKED AROUND to see if anyone else had slipped away from the party, to get some air, or maybe grab a smoke.

But no – he and Terry Crichton were alone. Harry waited for the pilot to react.

"Okay. I can see why you're worried," said Crichton.

"I only wish Amelia shared that view."

"You sure that O'Brien's telling the truth?"

"I don't know what to think."

"Indeed. But Albion? No love lost there with Sandbourne – but hard to believe they'd stretch to downright sabotage."

Harry knew that Terry Crichton was being honest.

But then, would he actually know if his paymasters were up to no good?

"Here's the thing, Harry. Don't want to stir anything up, but…" Harry wondered what Crichton was about to tell him, assuming he'd be warned about the man's affection for the bottle. "You see, O'Brien's a crack engineer all right. Was assigned to my last squadron in '17. Nothing about the planes that he *didn't* know, or couldn't figure out."

"Can see that myself. When steady, certainly good at his job."

Crichton nodded, and leading with his wounded leg, took a step closer.

"More than steady. Risked his life pulling one of my chaps out of his burning machine. Got a medal for it. Spent a year in hospital too."

"That had to be tough."

"Oh yes. Gets worse, though. Poor chap came back, but started to hit the bottle in a bad way. One night, took it out on someone in a bar. Court-martialled, got the book thrown at him. Lost his pension, the lot. Completely out on his ear."

Harry listened carefully – this story, sadly not so unusual.

"Heard a few years back he got into even more trouble, bit of petty theft here and there, and then, as we both know, that world of flying, well, *took off*."

"People prepared to hire him, look the other way?"

"Ha. Guess you could put it that way, Harry. And with O'Brien's talents, the man *was* needed. But I did hear that he always had some kind of money problem going on. Old debts, that sort of thing."

Harry suddenly knew where Crichton was going with this.

"So you're saying, look no further than O'Brien?"

"Fraid so. If someone offered him money to make things go wonky? Well, from what I hear, I doubt he'd refuse."

Harry nodded.

This – still no evidence that O'Brien had rigged the fuel gauge.

But it certainly made him question how wise it had been to trust the mechanic with guarding the *Firefly*.

"Thanks Terry. Looking forward to seeing you in the air tomorrow."

"And I'm looking forward to seeing the rather amazing Amelia."

"Yes – and now I'd best locate my wife."

"You two – quite the pair, eh Harry? More than just a mundane marriage with all the bells and whistles? You're a *team*."

And at that, Harry laughed as Terry walked back to the side entrance to the manor house, while he, with a nod, cut away, heading to the field where the planes and the pilots stood, waiting out the night.

KAT CREPT CLOSER to the side of the barn, still hugging the shadows, just yards away from the *Firefly*.

Close enough now, and she could see the figure, partly obscured by the plane, unaware that they were being watched.

What were they up to?

Whatever it was, Kat knew she couldn't wait any longer. This was the time to catch them red-handed – if there was anything to catch them at!

But before she could launch herself on them – a movement caught her eye in the shadow thrown by the plane's great engine, and she saw another figure rush towards the *Firefly*.

And then, the two shapes embraced.

And with a bit of a turn – after what was clearly a series of passionate kisses – the flickering light from the campfires hit the woman of the pair, her dress, her face.

Pidge. Amelia's sister. And now Kat had no doubt who the other figure was: Ronald Greene.

But as she debated what to do – whether she should go over to them, break up the party, maybe give the sleeping O'Brien a swift kick – she felt a sudden tap on her shoulder, startling, even frightening her.

And she spun around to see Harry, hidden in the dark as well.

"Well, you *do* know how to creep up on a girl, now, don't you?"

"Mandatory skill in a British lad's education. Say, isn't that—"

She saw that Harry had noted the pair next to the plane.

"Yeah. Mr Greene. Pidge. I had noticed he wasn't at the dinner. Found that odd. Guess this explains it."

"What we call an 'assignation'. Where's O'Brien?"

"Passed out – right over there."

"Damn," said Harry. "Must have got a bottle from one of the other ground crew."

"Think we should wake him?"

Harry shook his head.

"No. Dead to the world or not, with him lying there it's unlikely anyone will mess with the *Firefly*." She saw he took a breath. "At least, anyone *else*."

"What? You learn something about him?"

"*That I did*. Look – I think for now, it's best if Greene doesn't know we spotted him. Or O'Brien for that matter. Most important thing – somebody keeps a close eye on that plane tonight, right?"

"You mean us?" said Kat. "We can take shifts."

"Love your dedication! But no need. I just had a word with Huntley, explained the situation. He's on his way now, with one of the lads from the village. They'll keep guard through the night."

"Good for him."

"Beyond the call of duty," said Harry. "A good sort, to be sure." Then he smiled. "Though I do believe he's also taken a bit of a shine to our American guest."

"I'll bet he's not the only one."

"You think?"

102

"Oh, I'm sure. Quite gamine and all, the brave female pilot. Still – there is something about her, yes? Anyway – for now, for us – back to the Manor?"

"Absolutely."

"Good. You can tell me what your dashing pilot friend had to say about our sleeping engineer."

"You know that word 'dashing'? Not sure how one actually gets that label?"

"Oh, keep working at it. Like being a boy scout."

"Ah yes – merit badges and all that. And I imagine you give merit badges for a whole range of skills and activities?"

And as Harry put his arm around her, the night growing chilly, dew forming, pulling her close in the shadows, she laughed.

"Oh, that I do."

15.

THE AIR SHOW GOES ON

HARRY WAVED AWAY an offer of a cup a tea from one of the maids, all served from trestle tables on the grass overlooking the makeshift airstrip.

And he had to admit – despite their concerns and fears from last night – all this was so exciting, the display just a couple of hours away.

The planes being fuelled up, taxiing out from the stables into position, ready to attack the early morning sky.

A few of the wealthy and well-connected guests had also emerged to watch the preparations.

Harry suspected most of the others were still the worse for wear after so much bubbly the night before – pots of cash changing hands.

Kat came to his side, holding a plate of bacon sandwiches. She offered him one. He declined, with a smile.

"Sorry. Didn't we just have breakfast?" he said.

"Ha. Got these for Huntley and his pal," said Kat, gesturing to where the two lads now sat on the grass watching the activity.

"Sounds like they did a good job," said Harry.

He and Kat had got up early to relieve the night shift, taking it in turns to watch over the *Firefly* until O'Brien had woken and staggered off to bed to nurse his hangover.

"Nothing else to report?"

"Only that Huntley now says that *he* wants to be a flyer."

"Good for him," said Harry, laughing. "I'll take him up for a ride if I can borrow a two-seater."

"I *knew* you'd find an excuse to fly."

"Try and stop me," said Harry. He looked across at the stables where a small crowd had gathered around the *Firefly*.

"By the way – you see Amelia's turned up?"

"I did. Going to head over now."

"I see Smythe's there already, puffing on his cigar."

"The great impresario," said Kat.

At the far end of the line, he saw Terry Crichton checking out the *Bulldog*, ready to wait his turn for a practice run.

"Not many people out here yet," said Kat.

"Oh, give it another hour, there will be. I am sure Lavinia told the staff that they could all be out here too for this. Quite the event."

"Let's hope it stays a totally safe one."

And with that, she hurried down to the planes and Amelia.

WHEN KAT GOT there, she saw Amelia leaning against the side of the *Firefly*, listening dutifully to Smythe, the roly-poly man acting and sounding like he was the great mastermind of the spectacle to come.

To one side, Greene stood holding a lightweight camera in both hands, capturing the conversation – occasionally nudging onlookers to one side to get a better shot.

When Kat came close, she caught Amelia's eye. With a disarming smile, the aviatrix cut Smythe short and hurried to her side.

"Thanks for *saving* me," Amelia said, walking away from the plane, Smythe and Greene. But then a look of concern. "Anything wrong?"

Kat gestured towards the *Firefly*. "No sign of O'Brien yet?"

Amelia nodded quickly. "Oh, he'll surface, I'm sure."

Kat smiled, not wanting to alarm Amelia at all before the air show. So she said the next casually: "So you – you've done your own checks?"

"Oh, yes – made sure the fuel tanks are really full this time. Got one of the Sopwith crews to help me. Engine started over, all in good working order. Flaps, controls – also all good."

Then the aviatrix smiled and grabbed Kat's hands. "I'm *fine*, Kat. Nothing to worry about. But – want you to know – I appreciate the concern you and Sir Harry have."

Her smile broadened.

"Almost like family and – oh look – the first plane is taking off!"

And Kat turned to see a biplane begin to turn, ready to go full throttle down the grassy runway.

"Stay and watch the warm-ups with me?" Amelia said. "Another hour to kill before the show *really* starts."

Kat nodded, but also shot a look up at the hill. Harry standing with his pilot buddy; she was sure that he was being as observant as he could be.

"A Sopwith," Amelia said. "Something about those old planes. Listen to that engine! Such a great sound."

And Kat turned to stand with the world-famous woman next to her, and watched the vintage plane hurry and bounce along the grass, then claw into the air and arc across the blue sky.

"HARRY, IF YOU don't mind me saying so. You seem a little tense. The matter we discussed last night?"

Harry grinned. "Is it that obvious? Yes. We're worried."

Terry nodded in agreement. "Makes sense. But you know, a pilot like Amelia? She'll make sure that plane's in tip-top working order, regardless of her wobbly engineer."

"Yes. Expect so. Gosh, look at that Camel. I flew so many of those."

Terry turned to the air, the Sopwith arcing up, a beautiful sight in the morning sky, just with a few snow-white clouds hovering in the east.

"Yes. Though I must say, I do rather enjoy all the latest technological advances. These new machines? Practically fly themselves."

Harry laughed. "Whereas that one most definitely did not."

They stood and watched for a few more moments, Harry turning occasionally to scan the growing crowd on the lawn.

Many of the servants beginning to emerge too – the whole household given permission by Lavinia to watch the displays.

Not much longer now before the big event, he thought.

With all these people around, would anybody be fool enough to sabotage one of the planes?

He looked across at the *Firefly* over by the stables. Smythe standing proprietorially by the tail with a couple of Lavinia's guests, presumably explaining some technicality.

Kat and Amelia leaning together on the wing, laughing, chatting, watching the Sopwith chug across the sky. Kat saw him – gave a casual half wave.

All okay, he guessed it meant.

So far.

Slouched against the wall of the stables just yards from the *Firefly*, he saw Greene, camera over his shoulder, smoking – and deep in conversation with Pidge.

Where the hell's O'Brien? thought Harry. *Still in bed?*

Damn fool.

He just hoped the mechanic hadn't gone in search of a hair of the dog. He'd given strict instructions to Benton at breakfast that the staff were not to serve alcohol to O'Brien if he requested it.

Or even demanded it.

Another plane – an old Airco DH.2, it looked like – took off for its brief practice spin over the grounds of the property.

"Real thing starts in twenty, old chap," said Terry, checking his watch. "And before you know it, they'll be wanting me. Better get my kit on."

"Absolutely," said Harry. "And I must join my aunt for the opening flights. I promised to give some of her more wealthy guests a running commentary."

"Tales of derring-do?"

"I'll do my best."

"Of course! Anyway, must say, today's little display? Going to be quite the show. Do hope – amidst your worry – you get to enjoy it, even without flying?"

"Fly safe, Terry."

"Is there any other way?" the pilot answered, as he headed down to the *Bulldog*, ready to hit the blue sky in earnest.

HARRY WATCHED KAT come across the grass just as Terry got his *Bulldog* in line.

Lavinia's friends had listened intently as he'd given them an insider's take on the wartime role of the biplanes they now watched, twisting and turning in the sky above the manor.

Finally, as the display neared its end – and with only the *Bulldog* and the *Firefly* to go through their paces, the closing acts – he had managed to slip away to watch from the edge of the airstrip.

In the back of his mind throughout, a burning question: *Is Amelia going to be okay?*

One of the members of the local aviation club was serving as a flight director of sorts, armed with a red and green flag.

As Kat came abreast to him, the starter gave Terry a big wave of the green flag, and the *Bulldog* started bouncing down the grass, much more speedily than the planes that preceded it.

"Your friend's up," Kat said.

Harry nodded. "Between him and Amelia, think we're about to see some exciting flying."

Then Harry looked at her.

"Anything wrong, Kat? Amelia okay?"

"Oh, she's fine. Posing for more photos for Greene by the plane."

"Really? You'd think he'd have enough by now," said Harry. "Hey Kat – you sure you're okay?"

"Me? I'm a proper mess, I think is how'd you'd phrase it. O'Brien still hasn't turned up. I got one of the lads to check his quarters – not a sign of the man."

And Harry turned to her.

"Hang on – what?"

"Amelia said she thought he might be hobnobbing with the other pilots. But Harry, surely he should be right there, with her, no?"

"Definitely. He absolutely should be there for the final flight checks."

Now Harry scanned the crowd, both here, and the group of pilots and their mechanics huddled down by the field.

No damn O'Brien.

"Where the hell *is* he?"

He said that, not expecting an answer, but then he felt Kat's hand fly to his wrist.

"Harry. Wait a second. Look around. Absolutely everyone is out *here*."

"Right. Guests, staff, the lot—"

Then he could see exactly what thought had popped into Kat's mind.

"Ah, of course," said Harry. "The house is empty."

"And where did we find O'Brien yesterday?"

A quick nod. "In the pantry."

Kat had already started moving towards the house – away from the crowd with their heads all craned to the sky.

Harry followed his wife, saying, "Hate to miss all this."

"If we're right," said Kat, "it'll just be a question of dragging him out."

"And pouring a pot of coffee down him."

Following Kat, he took the stone steps up to the main house door two at a time.

16.

THE PANTRY

KAT, FREED OF last night's heels, retraced the path that led downstairs, to Benton's pantry.

She was moving so fast it was hard not to stumble down the ancient wood staircase, turning quickly down a corridor, not a soul in sight.

The kitchen staff all outside to watch the historic display.

She came to the almost shut door of the pantry, the yellow glow of a lamp showing from inside.

Slowly she pushed open the door, to see O'Brien.

But not at the table, with a bottle of whisky.

Instead, the mechanic crouched in the corner of the pantry, in front of the massive safe, leaning as close to the safe's tumblers as he could, as if still unaware that he wasn't alone.

Mumbling to himself.

She felt Harry at her side, and glanced at him quickly – his own face reflecting her surprise.

"I think, Mr O'Brien, you can stop right *there*."

O'BRIEN LURCHED round, eyes wide, trapped.

For one long stretch no one said anything.

Kat had to admit, *well, what does one say to a burglar interrupted in media res?*

Harry cleared his throat.

"Mr O'Brien, at this rather interesting juncture you have two *very* clear options."

The man's tongue licked at his lips. Had he had his morning constitutional? It certainly looked like it.

"You see," said Harry. "Amelia is about to take off, without you there, of course. Because you're here attempting to rob her of all the money that she raised."

"I, er, you don't *understand*—" said O'Brien getting to his feet.

Then Harry saw Kat raise a hand. He had to remind himself that she had worked in a New York criminal lawyer's office.

Kat could be – *when she wanted* – quite the intimidating presence.

"O'Brien, we have just witnessed you try to break into this safe. You cannot deny that. And I assume that it was you who sabotaged Amelia's fuel gauge the other day, hoping she'd crash?"

"That for money too?" Harry added quickly. "You see, as I said, you have two choices. Come totally clean with us. Or I will make sure they throw the whole damned book at you."

O'Brien seemed frozen.

Then Harry knew just the additional button to push.

"I know you got a bad deal. Losing your pension and all. I get that. You made some bad choices. And this right here? Well, it's not exactly petty theft. But if the sabotage was an attempt to kill Amelia—"

That spurred O'Brien as if he had been jolted with ends of electrical cables.

"No, no. Not at all. Didn't mean her any harm. I knew she could land that plane – dead engine. That's all. Just—" He hesitated, the dam about to break. "Just had to do it."

"For money."

O'Brien nodded. "Some. Not a lot."

Harry looked at Kat.

"But what about today?" she said, an absolute steely tone in her voice. "Is there any danger facing Amelia, the *Firefly*, *today?*"

He shook his head wildly. "No. None at all. Plane's in perfect shape." Then, as if reassuring himself. "She's fine."

"How the *hell* can you possibly know?" said Kat. "You've not even looked at the *Firefly* this morning!"

"I, er, gave her the once over yesterday. Everything – clean as a whistle."

Kat stared at the man. *Could they really believe him?*

She heard the sound of a plane, low over the house. That had to be Crichton in the *Bulldog*.

With Amelia yet to take off. But with O'Brien *AWOL*, was she safe?

Beside her, Harry took a breath.

"Like I said. I understand you got a rough deal, eh? Still all this has to come out. Who paid you to fix the fuel gauge?"

That seemed to stun the now quizzical looking O'Brien.

"You don't know that?"

"Enlighten us," said Harry.

"W-was that bastard Smythe."

"What?" said Kat.

"Smythe?" said Harry. "But why on earth would he—?"

"He wanted a bit of drama and excitement. Show off how good Amelia could be, even when something went wrong. He knew she could handle that situation, make for 'great press', he said."

Kat looked at Harry. They hadn't seen that coming.

The great impresario actually paying someone to mess with the plane?

Going to be a busy day for the local police, she thought.

"So Smythe. You just called him a 'bastard'," said Kat. "Why? He gave you work, didn't he?"

"Yeah, sure. But then he forced me do that nonsense with the fuel. And now, turns out — I found out! — he's gonna *fire* me when this is all over. Lay me off without a penny!"

If that's true? Then Smythe's one piece of work, all right, Kat thought.

"Well then," Harry said. "Seems to me, after all the planes are down, safe and sound, we shall have to have a little chat with Wallace Smythe, right? Of course the local constabulary will — I am sure — also be quite interested."

O'Brien's face finally fell. Whatever dream of a life he had after this, was now totally dashed. Even with Harry putting in an exculpatory word — about O'Brien's war service, his bad deal — still he'd be facing a good amount of jail time.

"But right now," she said. "We want you to get out to that field, help Amelia into the air." She took a breath. "Do your job."

"With the two of us looking over your shoulder," said Harry. "*Just in case* you get any ideas."

"One last question," said Kat, with a quick glance at Harry.

O'Brien turned to her.

"How did you even *think* you could crack a safe like this? I mean — without the combination — it's unbreakable."

O'Brien shuffled his feet, looked away. *Big hesitation right there,* she thought.

Something hidden.

"I dunno," he said uneasily. "Thought maybe, well, I'd get lucky."

Kat kept her eyes locked on his. Knowing the man was lying. He wouldn't have risked everything on getting lucky with the safe.

No question: he must have had some kind of inside info.

She looked at Harry, the same suspicious look on his face.

Both of us thinking the same thing, she thought.

What is O'Brien not telling us?

With Harry flanking the engineer on one side, they led him out of the pantry, up the stairs and out of the house, onto the great lawn.

Just in time to see Terry Crichton performing a beautiful low sweeping arc over the grounds, ready to land.

The main attraction up next: Amelia Earhart.

KAT STAYED CLOSE to Harry as they walked. She noticed that he kept a hand on O'Brien's shoulder, as if reminding him not to even *think* of getting away.

Though – given the alcohol on O'Brien's breath and the occasional stumble – she doubted the man would get far.

"Out of interest," said Harry to him, "just curious. Where did you get the booze last night? You steal that too?"

"No, I didn't!" said O'Brien, for once stirred enough to raise his voice. "I had a few drinks with Mr Greene! I didn't steal *nothing*!"

Funny, thought Kat. *She hadn't put Greene down as someone who'd stay up boozing with a mechanic.*

She noted, as Crichton finally levelled off, straightened out, and began bringing his plane down, that Amelia was already taxiing out to the grass runway.

"Dammit – we're too late," said Harry, shaking his head.

"Maybe she got some other crew to help?" said Kat. Then she turned to O'Brien. "That possible?"

"I – I dunno," said O'Brien, now looking nervous.

As they slowly made their way down to the planes, the *Bulldog* touched down as gently as could be.

Then, slowing, engine throttling down, the plane turned, facing the crowd.

As she and Harry and O'Brien passed the long line of onlookers, she saw Smythe standing with Pidge, beaming, glass of champagne in hand.

"Confront Smythe now?" she asked Harry.

"Don't know. You think… yes?"

"I think – let's see the air show off to its big finish, then, with Mr O'Brien here in tow, we corner him."

"Perfect – I'll also make sure Benton has rung up Sergeant Timms and Constable Thomas. Get them in on all the fun."

"Let's hope Smythe didn't come up with some other plan to add a little drama to the day," said Kat, seeing Amelia give a characteristic wave from her cockpit to the crowd.

Just then, a thought niggled at her: *Sure, Smythe's fuel trick had put the Firefly on the front pages.*

But how did he really benefit from that? Lavinia's air show tickets had sold out long ago.

It was Greene who'd made a fortune from all those covers – not Smythe.

And just then, she stopped dead in her tracks and looked across the airfield.

Crichton's *Bulldog* had returned to the plane parking lot, while at the end of the runway, the *Firefly's* engine note was rising, ready for take-off.

At the edge of the field, she spotted Greene adjusting a camera on a big tripod. A few yards away, he had another camera set up, pointing to the blue sky above.

"Harry," she said, ideas forming. Ideas becoming *suspicions.*

They were nearly at the stables, close to the other planes. O'Brien, his head down, looking about as guilty and hangdog as one could imagine.

Shamed, and perhaps fearing he was about to be destroyed.

Harry paused. "Okay. Kat – what is it?"

But it was O'Brien she turned   to.

"Back there, you said Smythe was going to sack you?" she said.

O'Brien nodded, looking nervous.

"Did Smythe tell you himself?"

"Well, no, but—"

"All right. So then – how do you know?" said Kat, stepping closer.

She saw O'Brien look across the grass, then back at her. *The unforeseen trap – sprung.*

"Let me hazard a guess. Greene told you – yes?" said Kat. "Last night. Right here."

"Maybe," said O'Brien. "Dunno. We had a couple of drinks."

"And some," said Harry.

"And – feeling lucky – let me try another guess," said Kat, catching Harry's eye, knowing he was already on board with this. "Greene also told you about the money in the safe, yes? Maybe how easy it would be to break into?"

"Bet he even gave you the combination too?" said Harry, joining in, following Kat's lead. "Told you he saw it the other day?"

"And suggested this morning would be the time to do it?" said Kat. "The house empty, Amelia getting ready to fly."

"The perfect time for you to get your revenge on Smythe," said Harry. "By pocketing his cash."

O'Brien visibly sagged as all this sunk in, as if – with Harry's hand on his shoulder – he had become a lifeless puppet.

She waited while Harry led the mechanic to the stables wall, and propped him up in the shade.

"Them damn numbers didn't work," O'Brien muttered, snapping. "The ones he gave me! Didn't bloody work at all."

Kat glanced at Harry as he returned.

Bingo! They were right – Greene had got O'Brien into a drunken stupor, and then fooled him into trying to crack the safe.

But that left one very big question: why?

"Harry," she said. "I don't get it. What was Greene up to?"

"I don't know. Maybe another story for him to sell? Country house robbery – war hero caught red-handed?"

Kat heard the *Firefly's* familiar engine roar, and she looked across at the runway: Amelia's plane had just leapt into the sky, moving at a sharp and steady angle into the wild blue.

But then a shout. She turned to see Crichton racing over, holding something in his hand.

"Sir Harry, Kat – coming in to land, I saw this, tossed in the grass. No one would see, I guess. But flying over, looking down, it caught the sun."

And at that moment he extended his gloved hand, holding a thick two-inch piece of steel.

"I think it's important," he said.

17.

THE RACE OF THEIR LIVES

KAT TOOK THE thick metal hex bolt. She had worked on her father's trucks and car back in the Bronx.

She knew – this was nothing from a tractor, or a car.

"O'Brien – what is *this*?"

The mechanic prised himself up and shuffled over, stared at the bolt.

"It's from the *Firefly*," he said, wiping his forehead as if he couldn't understand why Kat was holding it. "But that's impossible!"

"What do you mean – impossible?" said Harry. "What the *hell* part is it?"

"It's from one of the wing struts," said O'Brien, examining it more carefully. "Starboard assembly, I think. Yes."

"No," said Kat.

"Holds the bloody wing on," the mechanic said.

Kat was piecing things together fast.

"Wait," she said. "You mean it's somehow fallen off Amelia's plane?"

"Oh no. A part like this doesn't just *fall off*," said O'Brien. "Someone must have taken it off."

Ronald Greene, thought Kat instantly. *That job was easily done with O'Brien neatly out of the way.*

"Hang on," said Harry. "If Amelia tries that power dive…"

His voice trailed off, not saying the obvious.

Kat looked high into the sky, where Amelia was halfway through her routine.

The *Firefly*, climbing to a stall, then fluttering like a sycamore leaf towards the earth.

"*Amelia*," she said, her heart sinking.

She turned to Harry. "We have to warn her."

"From down here?" said Crichton. "There's no way."

But Harry was already quick off the mark, turning to the other pilot.

"Oh yes there is," he said. "The *Bulldog*."

"What?" said Crichton.

"Look, Terry, can I borrow the *Bulldog*? She's the only plane here that stands a chance of catching her."

"Go. Fast as you can, Harry."

But before Harry raced away, he turned to Kat.

"Greene," she said, anticipating what he was about to say.

"Damn right," said Harry.

"I'll deal with him."

She dangled the screw, then saw Harry take a silk handkerchief from his pocket and gesture to the bolt.

"Prints," he said.

She took the handkerchief and wrapped the bolt in it.

"Right. Kat, do what you can. Can't let that bastard get away."

And with that, Harry started running flat-out towards the *Bulldog*, the plane's team already preparing it to be moved away.

"Terry – can you keep an eye on Mr O'Brien here?" Kat said. "Despite his help just now, really don't want him slipping away."

But she paused just a moment to say to the hapless O'Brien,

"Thank you."

HARRY CLIMBED ONTO the wing of the *Bulldog*, where one of the fitters sat in the cockpit, preparing to taxi the plane to its final parking place.

"Sorry old chum," said Harry, grabbing Terry's jacket and leather helmet and putting them on. "Change of plan."

The mechanic obediently climbed out, and Harry slipped into the pilot's seat, strapping himself in.

One of the other mechanics started to question the move.

"Here now, just what—?"

Harry hit the throttle, and then shouted above the roar.

"Mr Crichton gave his okay. Bit of a flap on. Now – if you wouldn't mind removing the chocks?"

The man hesitated only a moment before, yanking away the twin blocks of wood to keep the plane from moving, and Harry immediately gunned the engine again.

The plane, its controls, its power – all new to him.

But not allowing himself a moment of doubt.

He absolutely had to do this.

KAT SKIRTED THE crowd – their eyes all on the skies, as up above Amelia did a perfect loop.

Then she hurried for Greene, the hex bolt in her hand.

She saw the photographer crouched over his camera, peering up into the sky, tracking the *Firefly*.

Waiting – she now knew – for Amelia's final dive, and that perfect shot, the dreadful, awful moment when her plane would break up, and his two cameras would capture the disaster.

And make him a fortune.

But while she was still well away, Greene, out of some instinct, turned and looked over. And Kat guessed it took him only that one look to figure out what was going on here.

The bolt in her hand. The evidence wrapped in silk.

Would he try and bluff his way out of it?

Kat knew that, for now, they had little concrete evidence. But all it needed was a single fingerprint – the magic of science – and Greene would be on a charge of attempted murder.

Life in prison.

"Mr Greene," she said, now just yards away. "A word."

Greene paused for a second, as if about to speak – then, panic in his eyes, he picked up the tripod and heavy camera, and hurled it at Kat.

She stumbled, fell, still clutching the bolt, her hip smashing into the hard ground – and saw Greene turn on his heels and run towards the house.

Groggy, Kat picked herself up – just as the *Bulldog* roared overhead and into the sky.

The sound of the engine kicking her into action.

Head down, shoes kicked off – she raced after Greene.

HARRY HELD THE stick tight as he saw the chimneys of Mydworth Manor fly past, barely a hundred feet below, and caught a glimpse of Kat running across the grass.

Been a while, he thought. *Can it really be like riding a bicycle? Planes have changed rather a lot over the years!*

The rudder controls were almost too responsive as he hurled the plane into a curving ascent to get to Amelia's altitude.

As for actually catching the Firefly?

Amelia was pushing the plane flat-out and Harry had no idea how fast the *Bulldog* could go.

He looked at the gauge showing the engine's **RPM**. One thing hadn't changed, he knew, since his own flying days: overwork an engine, and it could just blow.

But he had no choice now, and gave the throttle more power.

As to what he'd do when he caught her, he had no clue.

With the noise of her own plane, Amelia certainly wouldn't hear him tailing her.

Better just concentrate on catching her, Harry thought. *And even that won't be easy.*

AS KAT PICKED up her pace, a run now, Greene reached the gravel at the front of the house, where the cars were parked.

She saw him hop into the driver's seat of the yellow Rolls.

It started first time, and – with Kat still yards away – Greene dropped the handbrake and pulled out, the tail of the powerful car slewing gravel behind it.

Full speed past the house went the Rolls, nearly clipping some of the onlookers standing near the gravel driveway.

Damn, thought Kat, running full-tilt to where Harry had parked the Alvis.

Would it be up to the task of catching the Rolls?

She was about to find out.

She jumped into the Alvis, started it, and, flooring the pedal, spun the car in a near pinwheel circle to face down the driveway, and shot away in pursuit.

Clipping hedges and swerving awfully close to a tree, she saw the bright blotch of yellow ahead on the drive that led out of the estate and into the town.

She knew Greene would spot her in his rear-view mirror.

And when he saw her he'd only start driving the powerful car *even faster*.

Kat gripped the steering wheel tighter.

HARRY PAID NO attention to any of the gauges.

Full throttle now, and he was just a few hundred yards behind Amelia and – he thought – even beginning to gain a bit.

Fortunately, she hadn't yet reached the peak of her climb – the point where he knew she'd start her death-defying dive. Unaware that one wing was fatally weakened – ready to be ripped off as the plane tore through the air.

Harry used the rudder to get to the right of Amelia's plane, moving away from her slipstream. The *Bulldog* was struggling just to keep up with the *Firefly*.

He got a glimpse of Amelia, her face looking ahead, focused on what she had to do for her final, exhilarating display.

Just need a few more seconds, Harry thought.

Not knowing whether he'd actually get them.

KAT HAD SKIDDED through Mydworth's streets, a blur of people stepping aside, shouting, horses rearing, cars pulling over onto the pavement, angry horns tooting.

Now, out on the lane that led up onto the Downs, she realised that her years of driving the big concourse in the Bronx, and the new highways that had popped up leading to Long island, had done little to prepare her for high-speed driving in England.

It was beginning to feel like – forget about catching Greene – she'd be lucky not to go careering into a stone wall or a centuries-old tree.

And Greene definitely had the   advantage here.

He knew how to handle a car on these winding roads.

Kat pushed that thought away.

This was one criminal that she was not going to let get away.

FINALLY, WITH THE engine screaming, Harry was *there*, flying alongside the *Firefly*. Amelia looked over – her face looking stunned.

Harry knew that yelling was useless. Not over the roar of the two planes' engines.

But Amelia had seen him! He kept waving, making his hand point down, urging her as best he could: *Please don't do the final tricky manoeuvre that could rip the damn wing off!*

But Amelia didn't seem to understand.

Until Harry took a different tack, and pointed, as directly as he could, to the strut of the wing to Amelia's right.

Harry could see where one bolt was missing – the wing, even now, wobbling.

And with that, Amelia finally got it.

With a cheeky smile, and a tip to her pilot's cap, she began to slow, banking away, lowering the wounded plane to the ground.

Harry took a breath. *Have I taken a breath at all during the past few minutes?* he thought.

He turned to look at the fields far, far below, where amazingly, he saw two cars engaged in a crazy chase. The vehicles moving dots against the patchwork, but still instantly recognisable: the Yellow Rolls, as bold as the sun, and behind it his own dear Alvis.

And Harry knew his time in the air wasn't quite done.

KAT SAW THAT they'd hit a familiar stretch of the road, over gentle rolling hills – no trees clustered tight by the sides, just open fields and, in the distance, the brilliant sea.

Perfect to follow Greene, but also perfect for him to use the Rolls's power to keep the distance between them.

The Alvis was a good and speedy car.

But she couldn't gain on the Rolls.

Which is when she heard a sound, a rumble in the sky.

A plane.

She craned her neck round – to see the *Bulldog* swoop down behind her and then bank away, almost on its side.

What in the world is Harry planning? she thought.

HARRY QUICKLY TOOK in what was happening on this long stretch of road that swooped gently up and down, following the line of the Sussex Downs.

Greene was putting significant distance between himself and Kat.

Not much I can do about that from up here, he thought. *Or is there?*

KAT SAW HARRY, much lower now, fly right over her car. She could barely get a look at him as he gave her a thumbs up, the wings dipping.

A sign – she hoped – that Amelia was now safe!

Then the plane zoomed ahead, Kat still with the pedal floored, trying to guess what Harry was up to.

The *Bulldog* sailed over the Rolls too, racing ahead until it disappeared over the distant hill, dropping from sight completely.

"OKAY," HARRY SAID to himself as he brought the *Bulldog* round in the tightest of curves, using the whole valley, the engine racing.

He was about to do something he had certainly never done before.

He straightened up, now heading back the way he'd come, climbing up the slope of the valley, perfectly aligned with the empty road below, just feet above the hedges.

Almost low enough to land.

As he crested the rise out of the valley – there in the distance, racing towards him was the yellow Rolls-Royce, and behind it, Kat in the Alvis.

Barely a mile away. The closing speed of car and plane, he guessed… *maybe two hundred? Two-fifty?*

He kept that speed up as he barrelled straight at the yellow Rolls.

Every few seconds, closer until he could see Greene at the wheel.

Greene.

Willing to sacrifice Amelia for his own greed.

"All right then, let's see what you are made of, Mr Greene."

Harry kept his hands tight on the stick; the plane, just those few feet above the road, going even faster towards the yellow car.

KAT SAW THE insane move that Harry was trying here.

Back in her hometown, this game was played with cars – beat-up jalopies that no one cared about.

A game called "chicken".

And she knew one thing. If the game was "chicken", there was no way in hell her Harry would lose.

Least, that's what she hoped.

"COME ON, GREENE! Give it up! Otherwise, the two of us are going to make rather a large splash on this lovely road."

But it seemed like Greene wasn't slowing at all.

"Well, let's see then," Harry said.

With the car three hundred yards away – then two hundred – the distance closing fast, Harry felt that perhaps, for the next few seconds, breathing was optional.

When finally – so close that he could actually see Greene's terrified face – the Rolls veered sharply off the road, hit the grassy bank hard, and for a second became airborne…

… before smashing down in an absolutely perfect meadow and spinning to a halt – wreckage scattering among the tall grass.

In a corner of the field, a brown mare looked on. Surprised, Harry guessed, but thankfully unharmed.

Harry, knowing Kat was close behind, pulled the plane's nose up hard.

When he was up and level, he did one loop to see her out of the car with – yes – what looked like a revolver in her hand. Probably an unnecessary precaution – the battered Greene, slumped in the driving seat of the smashed Rolls, looked unlikely to be going anywhere soon.

On the road – in the distance – he saw a police vehicle.

And Harry thought: *Amelia's down, safe. Kat's safe. Greene about to face the police on one very serious charge – attempted murder. A nasty one.*

And then – then Harry laughed.

Thank God, he thought. *I'm still alive.*

Not a bad morning after all.

As he made one graceful circuit of the hilltop, gave a wave to his wife, then turned and headed back to Mydworth.

18.

BON VOYAGE

KAT CLINKED HER champagne flute against Amelia's and then Harry's.

A small army of servers on the first-class promenade deck of the Mauretania circled with frothy bottles of Perrier-Jouët.

So many people had wanted to see Amelia off on her journey back to America, but she had asked the two of them to stay behind for a private farewell.

"I say, Amelia, are you pleased?" Harry said." I mean with how things worked with the fundraising and all?"

"Oh yes. It will give our organisation a jump-start for sure! But I do feel bad that I didn't get to show what the *Firefly* could really do."

"I imagine that will all work out. I think Sandbourne will still get the contract. I'll tell you – in the *Bulldog*, I could barely catch you."

"And the others?" said Amelia. "Greene, Smythe…" – she made a significant pause here – "O'Brien?"

Kat took a sip of her bubbly. "Think they will be facing some serious problems, Amelia. As they should. Greene in particular."

At that, Amelia looked away.

"Yes. I know. Glad to see Greene put away."

"Pidge taking it okay?"

"Oh yes. She was, well, smitten. But she loves me dearly, and anyone who would hurt me, well—"

She trailed off.

"And Mr O'Brien? Somehow I feel bad for him."

"Well, they got Smythe for putting him up to the fuel tampering. But the attempted theft? That was all his."

"But he was so quick to identify the bolt. If he hadn't done that…"

Kat put a hand to her shoulder. This man had wanted to hurt Amelia, and yet here she was worrying about him.

"Yes, O'Brien. A sad case," said Kat.

"I'll put in a word," Harry said. "Know a few people in the courts. So yes, he's in for trouble – but I'll do what I can."

Amelia nodded, and she also took a big sip, finishing her champagne.

Which is when a white-gloved Cunard man walked nearby carrying a small three-note glockenspiel, which he hit with a steady rhythm before adding: "All ashore, going ashore!"

And Kat saw Amelia take a breath.

"Guess this is it. Listen, you two, you have to promise me, and soon – you'll come to New York together. We could have such great fun. Maybe bring your aunt as well?"

Harry laughed at that. "Oh, on that score, Lavinia would need no encouragement. Loves the 'colonies', as she calls them. And, well, I've never *really* seen Kat's hometown."

Amelia's grin widened. "Then it's a date, yes?"

Kat touched Amelia's shoulder again.

"Absolutely. My husband here is overdue for a look at what a big city is really like."

"That I am."

But then Kat detected a shift in Harry's voice.

"And Amelia, you must promise us something as well."

"Yes?"

"You have some big trips planned."

"Right. Soon, my solo flight across the Atlantic. Can't wait."

"Yes," Harry said. "Well, I... *we*... want you to take extra special care. To be safe, you know? You've become one of our dearest friends." Again, Harry's voice serious. "So, take care of yourself."

"I will."

And then as the man with the glockenspiel returned, those tones even more insistent.

"We best go," Kat said.

Amelia nodded, perhaps a bit of sadness in her eyes at the farewell. Then she gave Harry a big hug, and – when she finally released him – an even bigger one to Kat.

"Goodbye," she said.

"No, not goodbye," said Kat. "Au revoir."

At that, they turned to find the gangplank that led down to the dock at Southampton, the great RMS Mauretania ready to set sail across the Atlantic.

AND ON THE way down the gangplank...

"Well, I must admit," said Harry, "I'm a little emotional to see her go."

"Me too. Not the kind of person you meet every day of the week."

"That's for sure."

They stepped onto the dock, the enormous ropes starting to be undone from the great liner.

"What now? A drive in the country, roadside lunch, or—"

Kat took a second.

"Think... there's been a lot of excitement. Maybe back to Mydworth? I have some gardening to do."

"Ah yes, and I am *so* behind with the newspapers. Surely things have been going on in the world that I should be informed about."

He took her hand, as the ocean liner pulled away, and they saw Amelia up above, waving.

Amazing woman, Kat thought. *What else does life have in store for her?* That spirit, that fire, that sheer confidence...

Where would it all take Amelia Earhart?

NEXT IN THE SERIES:

THE WRONG MAN

MYDWORTH MYSTERIES #7

Matthew Costello & Neil Richards

When young Ben Carmody is found murdered in an alleyway one snowy night in Mydworth, all the evidence points to his best pal, Oliver. And though Oliver swears he is innocent, judge and jury are quick to convict the young man. But at the eleventh hour, Harry and Kat become involved, and aren't convinced.

With just days left before Oliver is to hang for the crime, they investigate. With the clock ticking can they find the real culprit in time ... to save a life?

ABOUT THE AUTHORS

Co-authors Neil Richards (based in the UK) and Matthew Costello (based in the US), have been writing together since the mid-90s, creating innovative television, games and best-selling books. Together, they have worked on major projects for the BBC, PBS, Disney Channel, Sony, ABC, Eidos, and Nintendo to name but a few.

Their transatlantic collaboration led to the globally best-selling mystery series, *Cherringham*, which has also been a top-seller as audiobooks read by Neil Dudgeon.

Mydworth Mysteries is their brand new series, set in 1929 Sussex, England, which takes readers back to a world where solving crimes was more difficult — but also sometimes a lot more fun.

CPSIA information can be obtained
at www.ICGtesting.com
Printed in the USA
BVHW072312050821
613452BV00005B/563